Retold Classics

NOVELS

Frankenstein

Huckleberry Finn

The Red Badge
of Courage

The Scarlet Letter

A Tale of Two Cities

Treasure Island

ANTHOLOGIES

American Classics,
Volume 1

American Classics,
Volume 2

American Classics,
Volume 3

American Hauntings

British Classics

Classic Chillers

Edgar Allan Poe

Jack London

Mark Twain

O. Henry

World Classics

The Retold Tales® Series features novels, short story
anthologies, and collections of myths and folktales.

Perfection Learning®

Contributing Writers

Michael A. Benware
B.A. English
English Teacher

Barbara L. Croft
Ph.D. English
Educational Writer

Debra Diane Felton
B.A. Communications
Educational Writer

Robert A. Klimowski
M.A. Reading, B.A. English
English Teacher

Beth Obermiller
M.A. English
Educational Writer

Michele Price
B.A. Communications
Educational Writer

Kristen L. Wagner
B.A. English
English Teacher

Mary J. Wagner
M.S. Reading, B.A. English
Reading Coordinator

Field Testers

Jon Ekstrand
Des Moines Alternative High
    School
Des Moines, Iowa

Janis Erwin
Kirby Junior High School
San Antonio, Texas

Gretchen Kauffman
Lincoln High School
Des Moines, Iowa

Ken Holmes
Lincoln High School
East St. Louis, Illinois

Michal Reed
Bartlett Junior High School
Springville, California

Retold Classics

AMERICAN
Classics
VOLUME 2

Perfection Learning®

Editors
Kathy Myers
Beth Obermiller

Book Design
Craig Bissell

Cover Illustration
Sue Cornelison

Inside Illustration
Paul Micich
Mark Bischel
Don Jonas

"The Secret Life of Walter Mitty," © 1942 James Thurber. © 1970 Helen W. Thurber and Rosemary A. Thurber. From *My World—and Welcome To It*, published by Harcourt Brace Jovanovich, Inc.

Adaptation of "The Lottery" from *The Lottery* by Shirley Jackson. © 1948, 1949 by Shirley Jackson. Copyright renewed © 1976, 1977 by Laurence Hyman, Barry Hyman, Mrs. Sarah Webster, and Mrs. Joanne Schnurer. Reprinted by permission of Farrar, Strauss and Giroux, Inc.

For information, contact
Perfection Learning® Corporation
1000 North Second Avenue, P.O. Box 500
Logan, Iowa 51546-0500.
Phone: 1-800-831-4190 • Fax: 1-800-543-2745
perfectionlearning.com

Paperback ISBN 0-8959-8131-9
Cover Craft® ISBN 0-8124-5461-8
20 21 22 23 24 PP 09 08 07 06 05

TABLE
OF CONTENTS

WELCOME TO THE RETOLD AMERICAN CLASSICS

Gone with the Wind, a '57 Chevy, blue jeans, and "Louie, Louie." What do this movie, car, piece of clothing, and song have in common? They're all great American classics.

We call something a classic when it is so well loved that it is saved and passed down to new generations. Classics have been around for a long time, but they're not dusty or out-of-date. That's because they are brought back to life by each new person who sees and enjoys them.

The *Retold American Classics* are stories written years ago that continue to entertain or influence today. The tales offer exciting plots, important themes, fascinating characters, and powerful language. They are stories that many people have loved to hear and share with one another.

RETOLD UPDATE

This book presents a collection of eight adapted classics. All the colorful, gripping, or comic details of the original stories are here. But longer sentences and paragraphs in the stories have been split up, and some old words have been replaced with modern language.

In addition, a word list has been added at the beginning of each story to make reading easier. Each word defined on that list is printed in dark type within the story. If you forget a word while you're reading, just check the list to review the definition.

You'll also see footnotes at the bottom of some pages. These notes identify people or places, explain ideas, or even let you in on an author's joke.

Finally, at the end of each tale you'll find a little information about the author. These revealing and sometimes amusing facts will give you insight into the writer's life and work.

When you read the Retold Tales, you bring each story back to life in today's world. We hope you'll discover why these Retold Tales have earned the right to be called American Classics.

THE SECRET LIFE OF WALTER MITTY

JAMES THURBER

VOCABULARY PREVIEW

Below is a list of words that appear in the story. Read the list and get to know the words before you start the story.

adjusted—arranged; put into correct position
attendant—person who is hired to do a service
bedlam—uproar; mad confusion
bickering—quarreling, especially about trivial things
complicated—difficult to understand or use
conquer—defeat; overpower
defendant—a person sued or accused in a court of law
derisive—mocking; scornful
disdainful—proud and scornful
distraught—very worried or upset
fleeting—passing; short-lived
hastily—quickly
inscrutable—mysterious; impossible to know or understand
inserted—put in, among, or between
insinuatingly—in a way that slyly hints or accuses
insolent—rude and haughty
intern—a student, especially a medical student, going through training
intimate—personal and private
menacing—threatening
vaulted—leaped

The Secret Life of Walter Mitty

James Thurber

Meet Walter Mitty. He's a meek, henpecked husband on a quest for puppy biscuits.

Then there's the other Walter Mitty: brave, noble, clever. He's the kind of hero that sparks dreams—especially for meek, henpecked husbands.

"We're going through!" The Commander's voice was like thin ice breaking. He wore his best uniform. His heavily braided white cap was pulled down in a sporty way over one cold gray eye.

"We can't make it, sir. It looks like a hurricane could whip up any minute, if you ask me."

"I'm not asking you, Lieutenant Berg," said the Commander. "Throw on the power lights! Rev her up to 8500! We're going through!"

continued

The pounding of the engine increased: ta-pocketa-pock-eta-*pocketa-pocketa*. The Commander stared at the ice forming on the pilot window. He walked over and twisted a row of **complicated** dials. "Switch on No. 8 backup!" he shouted.

"Switch on No. 8 backup!" repeated Lieutenant Berg.

"Full strength in No. 3 tower!" shouted the Commander.

"Full strength in No. 3 tower!"

Throughout the huge, rushing, eight-engined Navy seaplane, the crew looked at each other and grinned. "The Old Man'll get us through," they said to one another. "The Old Man ain't afraid of Hell" . . .

"Not so fast! You're driving too fast!" said Mrs. Mitty. "What are you driving so fast for?"

"Hmm?" said Walter Mitty. He looked at his wife in the seat beside him with shocked astonishment. She seemed extremely unfamiliar. She was like a strange woman who had yelled at him in a crowd.

"You were up to fifty-five," she said. "You know I don't like to go more than forty. You were up to fifty-five."

Walter Mitty drove on toward Waterbury in silence. The roar of the SN202, as it went through the worst storm in twenty years of Navy flying, faded into the deep, **intimate** airways of his mind.

"You're tensed up again," said Mrs. Mitty. "It's one of your days. I wish you'd let Dr. Renshaw look you over."

Walter Mitty stopped the car in front of the building where his wife went to have her hair done. "Remember to get those overshoes while I'm having my hair done," she said.

"I don't need overshoes," said Mitty.

She put her mirror back into her bag. "We've been all through that," she said, getting out of the car. "You're not a young man any longer."

He raced the engine a little.

"Why don't you wear your gloves? Have you lost your gloves?"

Walter Mitty reached in a pocket and brought out the gloves. He put them on. However, after she had gone into the building and he had driven to a red light, he took them off again.

"Pick it up, brother!" snapped a cop as the light changed. Mitty **hastily** pulled on his gloves and lurched ahead. He drove around the streets without any aim for a time. Then he drove past the hospital on his way to the parking lot.

. . . "It's the millionaire banker, Wellington McMillan," said the pretty nurse.

"Yes?" said Walter Mitty, removing his gloves slowly. "Who has the case?"

"Dr. Renshaw and Dr. Benbow. There are two specialists here, also: Dr. Remington from New York and Dr. Pritchard-Mitford from London. He flew over."

A door opened down a long, cool corridor and Dr. Renshaw came out. He looked **distraught** and worried. "Hello, Mitty," he said. "We're having a devil of a time with McMillan, the millionaire banker and close friend of President Roosevelt. He has obstreosis of the ductal tract.[1] Third-degree. Wish you'd take a look at him."

"Glad to," said Mitty.

In the operating room there were whispered introductions.

"Dr. Remington, Dr. Mitty. Dr. Pritchard-Mitford, Dr. Mitty."

"I've read your book on streptothricosis," said Prichard-Mitford as he shook hands. "A brilliant work sir."

"Thank you," said Walter Mitty.

"Didn't know you were in the States, Mitty," grumbled Remington. "It's like taking coals to Newcastle[2] to bring Mitford and me up here for an emergency."

"You are very kind," said Mitty.

---

[1] 1The medical terms in this section—"obstreosis," "ductal tract," "streptothricosis," and "coreopsis"—are nonsense.

[2] Newcastle is a coal center. To take coals to Newcastle would be to do something unnecessary.

continued

A huge, complicated machine sat next to the operating table. The machine and the table were connected by many tubes and wires. At this moment it began to go pocketa-pocketa-pocketa-pocketa.

"The new ansthetizer[3] is breaking down!" shouted an **intern**. "There is no one in the East who knows how to fix it!"

"Quiet, man!" said Mitty, in a low, cool voice. He sprang to the machine, which as now going pocketa-pocketa-queep-pocketa-queep. He began fingering gently a row of glistening dials.

"Give me a fountain pen!" he snapped. Someone handed him a fountain pen. He pulled a broken piston out of the machine and inserted the pen in its place.

"That will hold for ten minutes," he said. "Get on with the operation."

A nurse hurried over and whispered to Renshaw. Mitty saw the man turn pale. "Coreopsis has set in," said Renshaw nervously. "Would you take over, Mitty?"

Mitty looked at him and at the frightened figure of Benbow, who drank too much. Then he looked at the grave, uncertain faces of the two great specialists.

"If you wish," he said. They slipped a white gown on him. He **adjusted** a mask and drew on thin gloves. Nurses handed him shining . . .

"Back it up, Mac! Look out for that Buick!"

Walter Mitty jammed on the brakes.

"Wrong lane, Mac," said the parking-lot **attendant**. He looked at Mitty closely.

"Gee. Yeh," muttered Mitty. He began cautiously to back out of the lane marked "Exit Only."

"Leave her sit there," said the attendant. "I'll put her away."

Mitty got out of the car.

"Hey, better leave the key."

---

[3] An ansthetizer would dull pain or put a patient to sleep.

"Oh," said Mitty. He handed the man the key. The attendant **vaulted** into the car. He backed it up with **insolent** skill and put it where it belonged.

They're so damn cocky, thought Walter Mitty as he walked along Main Street. They think they know everything.

Once he had tried to take his chains off outside New Milford. He had got them wound around the axles. A man had had to come out in a wrecker and unwind them, a young, grinning garageman. Since then Mrs. Mitty always made him drive to the garage to have the chains taken off.

The next time, he thought, I'll wear my right arm in a sling. They'll see I couldn't possibly take the chains off myself.

He kicked at the slush on the sidewalk. "Overshoes," he said to himself and he began looking for a shoe store.

He came out onto the street later with the overshoes in a box under his arm. Walter Mitty then began to wonder what the other thing was his wife had told him to get. She had told him twice before they set out from their house for Waterbury.

In a way he hated these weekly trips to town. He was always getting something wrong. Kleenex, he thought, Squibb's, razor blades? No. Toothpaste, toothbrush, bicarbonate, carborundum, initiative and referendum?[4]

He gave it up. But she would remember it. "Where's the what's-its-name?" she would ask. "Don't tell me you forgot the what's-its-name."

A newsboy went by shouting something about the Waterbury trial.

... "Perhaps this will refresh your memory." The District Attorney suddenly pushed a heavy automatic pistol at the quiet person on the witness stand. "Have you ever seen this before?"

---

[4] Mitty is simply associating words that sound alike. Carborundum is a polish. Initiative and referendum are part of a voting process for laws.

continued

Walter Mitty took the pistol and examined it expertly. "This is my Webley-Vickers 50.80," he said calmly.

An excited buzz ran around the courtroom. The Judge rapped his gavel for order.

"You are a crack shot with any sort of gun, I believe?" said the District Attorney, **insinuatingly**.

"Objection!" shouted Mitty's attorney. "We have shown that the **defendant** could not have fired the shot. We have shown that his right arm was in a sling on the night of the fourteenth of July."

Walter Mitty raised his hand briefly. The **bickering** attorneys were silenced. "With any known type of gun," he said calmly, "I could have killed Gregory Fitzhurst at three hundred feet *with my left hand*."

Wild confusion broke loose in the courtroom. A woman's scream rose above the noise of the **bedlam**. Suddenly a lovely, dark-haired girl was in Walter Mitty's arms. The District Attorney struck at her savagely. Without rising from his chair, Mitty let the man have it on the point of the chin. "You miserable dog!" . . .

"Puppy biscuit," said Walter Mitty. He stopped walking. The buildings of Waterbury rose up out of the misty courtroom and surrounded him again. A woman who was passing laughed.

"He said 'Puppy biscuit,' " she said to her companion. "That man said 'Puppy biscuit,' to himself."

Walter Mitty hurried on. He went into an A. & P. He did not enter the first one but went into a smaller one farther up the street.

"I want some biscuits for small, young dogs," he said to the clerk.

"Any special brand, sir?"

The greatest pistol shot in the world thought a moment. "It says 'Puppies Bark for It' on the box," said Walter Mitty.

His wife would be through at the hairdresser's in fifteen minutes, Mitty saw in looking at his watch. But they might have trouble drying her hair. Sometimes they had trouble drying it. She didn't like to get to the hotel first. She would want him to be there waiting for her as usual.

He found a big leather chair in the lobby, facing a window. He put the overshoes and the puppy biscuits on the floor beside the chair. Then he picked up an old copy of *Liberty* magazine and sank down into the chair.

"Can Germany **Conquer** the World Through the Air?" Walter Mitty looked at the pictures of bombing planes and of ruined streets.

. . . "The bombing has young Raleigh on edge, sir," said the sergeant. Captain Mitty looked up at him through mussed hair.

"Get him to bed," he said wearily. "With the others. I'll fly alone."

"But you can't, sir," said the sergeant anxiously. "It takes two men to handle that bomber. The Archies[5] are pounding the hell out of the air. Von Richtman's circus[6] is flying between here and Saulier."

"Somebody's got to get that ammunition storehouse," said Mitty. "I'm going over. Bit of brandy?"

He poured a drink for the sergeant and one for himself. War thundered and whined around the dugout and pounded at the door. There was a tearing of wood and splinters flew through the room.

"A bit of a near thing," said Captain Mitty calmly.

"The bombers are closing in on all sides," said the sergeant.

"We only live once, Sergeant," said Mitty, with his faint, **fleeting** smile. "Or do we?" He poured another brandy and tossed it down.

[5]Archies is slang for antiaircraft guns.
[6]Mitty's Richtman is probably inspired by Baron Manfred von Richthofen (1892-1918). Richthofen was a German military leader during WWI. He led a group of fighter planes, which were known as "flying circuses."

"I never see a man could hold his brandy like you, sir," said the sergeant. "Begging your pardon, sir."

Captain Mitty stood up and strapped on his huge Webley-Vickers automatic. "It's forty kilometers through hell, sir," said the sergeant.

Mitty finished one last brandy. "After all," he said softly, "what isn't?"

The pounding of the cannon increased. There was the rat-tat-tatting of machine guns. And from somewhere came the **menacing** pocketa-pocketa-pocketa of the new flame-throwers.

Walter Mitty walked to the door of the dugout humming "Aupres de Ma Blonde."[7] He turned and waved to the sergeant. "Cheerio!" he said . . .

Something struck his shoulder. "I've been looking all over this hotel for you," said Mrs. Mitty. "Why do you have to hide in this old chair? How did you expect me to find you?"

"Things close in," said Walter Mitty vaguely.

"What?" Mrs. Mitty said. "Did you get the what's-its-name? The puppy biscuits? What's in that box?"

"Overshoes," said Mitty.

"Couldn't you have put them on in the store?"

"I was thinking," said Walter Mitty. "Does it ever occur to you that I am sometimes thinking?"

She looked at him. "I'm going to take your temperature when I get you home," she said.

They went out through the revolving doors that made a faintly **derisive** whistling sound when you pushed them. It was two blocks to the parking lot.

At the drugstore on the corner she said, "Wait here for me. I forgot something. I won't be a minute."

She was more than a minute. Walter Mitty lighted a cigarette. It began to rain—rain with sleet in it. He stood

[7]This was a popular French song during WWI. The title in English is "Close to My Blonde."

up against the wall of the drugstore, smoking . . . He put his shoulders back and his heels together.

"To hell with the handkerchief," said Walter Mitty scornfully. He took one last drag on his cigarette and snapped it away. Then, with that faint, brief smile on his lips, he faced the firing squad. He stood tall and motionless, proud and **disdainful**. Walter Mitty the Undefeated, **inscrutable** to the end.

"The Secret Life of Walter Mitty" was first published in 1942.

INSIGHTS INTO
JAMES THURBER

(1894-1961)

Thurber was a famous cartoonist as well as an author. E.B. White, Thurber's friend and co-worker at *The New Yorker* magazine, was one early admirer of Thurber's sketches. White insisted they were good enough to publish.

So White pulled them out of Thurber's wastebasket. Then he took them to the editor, Harold Ross. One cartoon actually made it onto the cover of the magazine.

Thurber's real triumph with cartoons at *The New Yorker* came later. In 1929, *Is Sex Necessary?* was published. Thurber cowrote and illustrated the book with White. The cartoons were a smash hit.

Ross soon appeared in Thurber's office. He demanded one of Thurber's sketches that he had turned down earlier.

Thurber said he had thrown the cartoon away.

Ross shouted, "Well, don't throw things away just because I reject them! Do it over again."

Thurber kept Ross waiting for two years.

When Thurber went to England in 1958, he received a high honor. The editors of *Punch* magazine asked him to sign their table.

Great English writers such as Thackeray had signed this table before. But the last American who had been asked was Mark Twain.

Dogs often appeared in Thurber's tales and cartoons. The link between Thurber and dogs became firm in the mind of readers. Many wrote asking Thurber to name their pets.

continued

Thurber was not flattered by the requests. He wrote back that dog names were at 176th place on his list of fascinating things.

Thurber continued to fight the image of a dog-lover. However, he did own many dogs. Poodles were his favorite. By 1955, he had had over twenty-five for pets.

In a childhood game, Thurber was blinded in his left eye by an arrow. During the last fifteen years of his life, he was almost totally blind. He continued to write with the help of his wife, Helen.

Thurber was also aided by his great memory. He could write entire stories in his head. Thurber proved his ability while a psychology student at Ohio State. His class was asked to write down what they could remember of a 1000-word article. Thurber's recall was 78%—far better than anyone else who took the test.

Other works by Thurber:
    "The Catbird Seat," short story
    Fables for Our Time, book
    My Life and Hard Times, autobiography
    The Male Animal, play, cowritten with Elliott Nungent
    The Thurber Carnival, book

THE OUTCASTS OF POKER FLAT

BRET HARTE

VOCABULARY PREVIEW

Below is a list of words that appear in the story. Read the list and get to know the words before you start the story.

abated—died down; decreased
advisable—wise; worth being suggested as a plan of action
amiability—pleasantness and friendliness
banishment—forced removal from one's own country; exile
compelled—forced to do something
defection—desertion of one's country, group, friends, etc.
exiles—people forced to leave their own land; outcasts
intimidation—the act of influencing someone by using scare tactics
irrelevance—the quality of being unrelated or not appropriate
malevolence—spite; ill will
notorious—famous (especially in a negative way)
permanently—in a lasting way
persisted—continued on
philosophic—calmly sensible, accepting bad luck without deep emotion
professional—relating to an occupation
rations—fixed portion (usually food) granted to one person
rigid—stiff and unbending
seclusion—aloneness; being separated from others
tact—skill and smoothness in dealing with people and situations
vernacular—common, everyday speech

THE
OUTCASTS
OF
POKER
FLAT

*John Oakhurst, gambler, knows about luck.
Stuck in the wilds with some fellow outcasts,
Oakhurst can tell he's in a bad streak.
Then unexpected visitors appear at the
outcasts' camp. Their arrival may not improve
the outcasts' luck, but the players are in
for some changes.*

Mr. John Oakhurst, gambler, stepped into the main street of Poker Flat on the morning of November 23, 1850. As he did so, he scented a change in the moral atmosphere since the night before.

Two or three men were talking seriously together. They stopped as he approached and traded meaningful glances.

BRET HARTE

There was a Sabbath[1] quiet in the air. In a settlement not used to Sabbaths, this seemed threatening.

Mr. Oakhurst's calm, handsome face showed small concern about these signs. Whether he knew of any cause was another question.

"I reckon they're after somebody," he reflected. "Likely it's me."

He finished whipping away the red dust of Poker Flat from his neat boots. Then he returned his handkerchief to his pocket. With that, he quietly put aside any further guesses.

In fact, Poker Flat was "after somebody." It had lately lost several thousand dollars, two valuable horses, and an important citizen. Now it was reacting with a fit of virtue.

This reaction was as lawless and wild as any act that had provoked it. A secret committee had decided to rid the town of all improper persons.

In the case of two men, this had been done **permanently**. They had been hanged from the branches of a tree in the gulch.[2]

Other less permanent measures had been taken. The **banishment** of certain undesirable characters had been announced. I regret to say that some of these were ladies.

But, in defense of females, it should be said that their improper behavior was **professional**.[3] And Poker Flat dared to sit in judgment only on such easily set standards of evil.

Oakhurst was right in guessing that he was one of the improper persons. A few of the committee had urged hanging him as an example. This also would have been a sure method of getting back the sums he had won from them.

"It's agin justice," said Jim Wheeler. "We can't let this here young man from Roaring Camp carry away our money. And an entire stranger, at that."

---

[1] A Sabbath is a day set aside by some religions for rest and worship.
[2] A gulch is a small canyon.
[3] The women are prostitutes.

But there was a crude sense of justice among some who had been lucky enough to win from Mr. Oakhurst. They overruled the more narrow-minded people.

Mr. Oakhurst received his sentence with **philosophic** calm. Not even the hesitation of his judges shook his coolness. He was too much of a gambler not to accept fate. With him, life was at best an uncertain game. He recognized the usual odds in favor of the dealer.

A body of armed men went with the banished group to the outskirts of town. The armed party was present for the **intimidation** of Oakhurst. He was known to be a coolly desperate man.

Besides Mr. Oakhurst, there was a young woman commonly known as The Duchess. Another woman, given the unfortunate title of Mother Shipton,[4] was also in the party. And there was Uncle Billy. He was suspected of robbing sluices[5] and known to be a drunkard.

The parade of people did not stir any comments from those who watched. Nor was any word uttered by the armed men.

Finally they reached the gulch that marked the outer limit of Poker Flat. Only then did the leader speak briefly and to the point. The **exiles** were forbidden to return at the peril of their lives.

As the escort disappeared, the exiles vented their feelings. The Duchess shed a few wild tears. Mother Shipton used some bad language. Uncle Billy shot a string of swear words as he retreated.

The philosophic Mr. Oakhurst alone remained silent. He listened calmly to Mother Shipton's desire to cut somebody's heart out. He also listened to the Duchess often repeat that she would die on the road. And he took in the alarming oaths that seemed to be bumped out of Uncle Billy as he rode.

---

[4]Mother Shipton was the name of an English woman accused of witchcraft.

[5]Uncle Billy was suspected of stealing gold. A sluice is a channel for carrying off water. Gold miners used sluices to wash gold from dirt.

Mr. Oakhurst had the easy good nature of most gamblers. This led him to insist upon giving his own riding horse, Five-Spot, to the Duchess. In exchange, he took the miserable mule which she rode.

But even this act did not draw the party any closer. The young woman readjusted her tattered plumes with a feeble, faded, flirting air. Mother Shipton eyed Five-Spot's rider with **malevolence**. And Uncle Billy swore at the whole party in one sweeping curse.

The outcasts knew of a camp called Sandy Bar which had not yet experienced the reforming influences of Poker Flat. That camp seemed inviting to the travelers.

However, the road to Sandy Bar lay over a steep mountain range. It was as distant as a hard day of travel. In that late season, the party soon left the moist, mild foothills. The dry, cold, bracing air of the Sierra Mountains awaited them.

The trail was narrow and difficult. At noon the Duchess rolled out of her saddle upon the ground. She declared she did not intend to go any farther. So the party halted.

The spot was particularly wild and impressive. They had stopped in an arena formed by the woods. This was circled on three sides by steep cliffs of naked granite. The fourth side sloped gently up to another cliff that overlooked the valley.

It was undoubtedly the most suitable spot for a camp— if camping had been **advisable**. But Mr. Oakhurst knew that they had covered scarcely half the distance to Sandy Bar. And the party was not equipped or supplied for delay.

He briefly pointed out this fact to his companions. He added a philosophic remark on "throwing up their hand before the game was played out."

But they had liquor. In this emergency, drink made up for food, fuel, rest, and insight.

In spite of his protests, they were soon more or less under its influence. Uncle Billy passed rapidly from anger into a daze. The Duchess became weepy. Mother Shipton snored.

Mr. Oakhurst alone remained on his feet. He leaned against a rock and calmly surveyed them.

Oakhurst did not drink. It interfered with his profession. Gambling required coolness, controlled emotions, and an alert mind. In his own words, he "couldn't afford it."

As he gazed at his fellow exiles, Mr. Oakhurst felt seriously troubled for the first time by his life. The loneliness of his scorned trade, his habits, even his vices bothered him.

Oakhurst dusted his black clothes and washed his hands and face. As he busied himself with these typical neat habits, he forgot his annoyance. Perhaps the thought of deserting his weaker, more pitiful companions never occurred to him.

Yet he could not help feeling a lack of excitement. Oddly enough, excitement helped him maintain that calmness for which he was **notorious**.

Mr. Oakhurst looked at the gloomy walls. They rose a thousand feet steeply above the circling pines around him. He stared at the threatening, clouded sky. Then he stared at the valley below, already becoming shadowy. Doing so, he suddenly heard his own name called.

A horseman slowly came up the trail. Mr. Oakhurst recognized the fresh, open face of the newcomer. It was Tom Simson, otherwise known as The Innocent, of Sandy Bar.

Mr. Oakhurst had met him some months before over a "little game." With perfect calmness, he had won the entire fortune ($40) of that simple youth.

The game finished. Then Mr. Oakhurst pulled the youthful bettor behind the door.

He said to him, "Tommy, you're a good man. But you can't gamble worth a cent. Don't try it again."

He then handed Tom his money back and pushed him gently from the room. By so doing, he made a devoted slave of Tom Simson.

Tom's boyish and enthusiastic greeting of Mr. Oakhurst showed he remembered the incident. Tom said he had started out for Poker Flat to seek his fortune.

"Alone?"

No, not exactly alone. In fact (he giggled), he had run away with Piney Woods. Didn't Mr. Oakhurst remember Piney? The one who used to wait on the table at the Temperance House?[6]

They had been engaged a long time. But old Jake Woods had objected, so they ran away. They were going to Poker Flat to be married. And here they were!

And they were tired out. How lucky it was they had found a place to camp. How lucky to find company.

The Innocent delivered all this rapidly. Meanwhile, Piney—a plump, pretty girl of fifteen—emerged from behind a pine tree. She had been there all the time, blushing as she hid. Piney rode to the side of her lover.

Mr. Oakhurst seldom troubled himself with sentiment and still less with proper behavior. But he had a vague idea that the situation was not fortunate.

He still had some presence of mind, however. He managed to kick Uncle Billy, who was about to say something. And Uncle Billy was sober enough to feel a superior power in that kick that should not be crossed.

Mr. Oakhurst then tried to persuade Tom Simson not to delay anymore. But his arguments were in vain. He even pointed out that there were no supplies and no means of making a camp.

But, unluckily, the Innocent met this objection. He assured the party that he had an extra mule loaded with supplies. He had also discovered a crudely built log house near the trail.

---

[6]Temperance Houses were hotels where liquor was not served.

"Piney can stay with Mrs. Oakhurst," said the Innocent, pointing to the Duchess. "And I can make do for myself."

Only Mr. Oakhurst's warning foot saved Uncle Billy from bursting into a roar of laughter. As it was, Uncle Billy felt **compelled** to retreat to the canyon until he could keep a straight face. There he told the joke to the tall pine trees. He repeated it with many slaps of his leg, twistings of his face, and the usual swearing.

But when he returned, he found the party in apparently friendly conversation. The air had grown strangely chill and the sky overcast. So the group was seated by a fire.

Piney was actually talking in an open, girlish fashion to the Duchess. And the Duchess was listening with an interest and liveliness she had not shown in many days.

The Innocent was talking to Mr. Oakhurst and Mother Shipton. His words were apparently having the same effect as Piney's. The lady actually seemed to be relaxing into **amiability**.

"Is this here a d- - - -d[7] picnic?" said Uncle Billy to himself with scorn. He surveyed the group, the dancing firelight, and the tied animals nearby.

Suddenly an idea mingled with the alcohol that disturbed his brain. It was apparently a humorous one. He felt he had to slap his leg again and cram his fist into his mouth.

The shadows crept slowly up the mountain. A slight breeze rocked the tops of the pine trees and moaned down their long, gloomy aisles. The ruined cabin, patched and covered with pine branches, was set apart for the ladies.

As the lovers parted, they innocently kissed. It was such an honest and sincere kiss that it might have been heard above the swaying pines.

The frail Duchess and malevolent Mother Shipton were probably too stunned to remark about this last sign of simplicity. So they turned without a word to the hut.

[7]In the past, words that might have offended readers were often blanked out. Billy is saying "damned."

Fuel was added to the fire. The men lay down before the door. They were asleep in a few minutes.

Mr. Oakhurst was a light sleeper. Toward morning he woke numb and cold. He stirred the dying fire. As he did so, the strong wind brought to his cheek something that made his blood leave it. Snow!

He jumped to his feet, intending to awaken the sleepers. There was no time to lose! But turning to where Uncle Billy had been lying, he found him gone.

A suspicion leaped to his brain and a curse to his lips. He ran to the spot where the mules had been tied. They were no longer there. The tracks were already rapidly disappearing in the snow.

The excitement brought Mr. Oakhurst back to the fire with his usual calm. He did not waken the sleepers.

The Innocent slept peacefully. There was a smile on his good-humored, freckled face.

The virgin Piney slept beside her frailer sisters. She rested as sweetly as though she were guarded by heavenly angels.

Mr. Oakhurst drew his blanket over his shoulders. He stroked his mustaches and waited for the dawn.

Daybreak came slowly in a whirling mist of snowflakes that dazzled and confused the eye. What could be seen of the landscape appeared magically changed.

Mr. Oakhurst looked over the valley. He summed up the present and future in two words: "Snowed in!"

The supplies were carefully checked. Fortunately for the party, these had been stored within the hut. They had therefore escaped Uncle Billy's thieving fingers. They found that with care and wisdom they might last ten days longer.

"That is," said Mr. Oakhurst in an undertone to the Innocent, "if you're willing to feed us. If you ain't—and perhaps you'd better not—you can wait until Uncle Billy gets back with supplies."

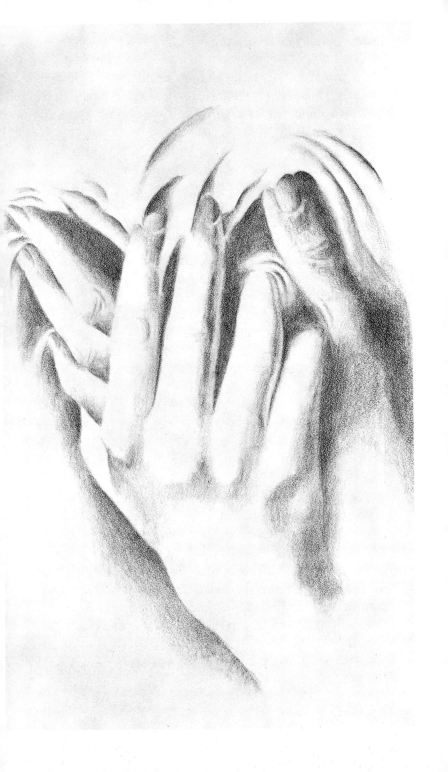

For some secret reason, Oakhurst could not bring himself to reveal Uncle Billy's villainy. So he suggested that Uncle Billy had wandered from camp and accidentally stampeded the animals.

He dropped a warning to the Duchess and Mother Shipton. Of course they knew the facts of their companion's **defection**.

"They'll find out the truth about us *all* when they find out anything," he added in a meaningful tone. "And there's no good frightening them now."

Tom Simson made all his worldly store available to Mr. Oakhurst. He actually seemed to enjoy the thought of their forced **seclusion**.

"We'll have a good camp for a week. Then the snow'll melt, and we all go back together."

The young man's cheerfulness and Mr. Oakhurst's calm infected the others. The Innocent fixed a roof for the cabin with the aid of pine branches.

Meanwhile, the Duchess directed Piney in rearranging the inside. Her taste and **tact** opened the eyes of the country maiden to their widest.

"I reckon now you're used to such fine things at Poker Flat," said Piney.

The Duchess turned away sharply. She seemed to be trying to hide something. Her cheeks turned red under her heavy makeup. Mother Shipton requested Piney not to "chatter."

But when Mr. Oakhurst returned from a weary search for the trail, he heard the sound of happy laughter echoed from the rocks. He stopped in some alarm. His thoughts first naturally went back to the whiskey. He had wisely hidden it.

"And yet it don't somehow sound like whiskey," said the gambler.

He caught sight of the blazing fire and the group around it through the still blinding storm. This finally convinced him that it was "square fun."

Whether Mr. Oakhurst had hidden away his cards with the whiskey, I cannot say. However, in Madam Shipton's words, he "didn't say 'cards' once" during that evening.

As it happened, the time was whiled away by an accordion. Tom Simson had produced this with somewhat of a showy air. Piney Woods had some difficulties working this instrument. But she managed to pluck several creeky tunes from its keys. The Innocent accompanied her with a pair of bone castanets.[8]

The crown of the merrymaking that evening was a simple hymn. The lovers, joining hands, sang the song very earnestly and loudly.

I fear it was not the holy quality of the hymn that speedily inspired the others. Rather it was the song's brave tone and swinging rhythm that led them to join in.

"I'm proud to live in the service of the Lord,
And I'm bound to die in His army."

The pines rocked and the storm swirled and whirled above the miserable group. The flames of their altar leaped heavenward, as if a sign of their vow.

At midnight the storm **abated**. The rolling clouds parted. The stars could be seen glittering keenly above the sleeping camp.

Mr. Oakhurst's professional habits let him live on the smallest possible amount of sleep. In dividing the watch with Tom, he somehow managed to take the greater part of that duty. He explained to the Innocent that he had "often been a week without sleep."

"Doing what?" asked Tom.

---

[8]Castanets, a musical instrument, are shaped like two flat shells. When struck together with the fingers, they make a clicking sound.

"Poker!" replied Oakhurst crisply. "When a man gets a streak of luck—red-hot luck—he don't get tired. The luck gives out first.

"Luck," continued the gambler thoughtfully, "is a mighty strange thing. All you know about it for certain is that it's bound to change. And it's finding out when it's going to change that makes you.

"We've had a bad streak of luck since we left Poker Flat. You came along and—slap—you get into it, too.

"If you can hold your cards right along, you're all right. For," he added with cheerful **irrelevance**,

"I'm proud to live in the service of the Lord,
And I'm bound to die in His army."

The third day came. The sun looked through the white-curtained valley. It watched as the outcasts divided their slowly decreasing supplies for the morning meal.

It was one of the odd things about that climate that the sun spread kind warmth over the wintery landscape. It was as if the land regretted the past and sympathized with the outcasts.

But the sun also revealed drift on drift of snow piled high around the hut. A hopeless, uncharted, trackless sea of white lay below the rocky shores to which the castaways clung. Through the marvelously clear air, the smoke of Poker Flat rose miles away.

Mother Shipton saw it. From a peak of her rocky perch, she hurled a final curse in that direction. It was her last attempt at swearing. Perhaps for that reason, it was great to a certain degree.

It did her good, she privately informed the Duchess. "Just you go out there and cuss and see."

She then set herself to the task of amusing "the child." That was what she and Duchess were pleased to call Piney.

Piney was no chicken. But the pair held that soothing and original theory about her. They needed to account for the fact that she didn't swear and wasn't improper.

Night crept up again through the canyons. The reedy notes of the accordion rose and fell in fits and long gasps by the flickering campfire.

But music failed to entirely fill the aching emptiness left by skimpy meals. A new entertainment was proposed by Piney—storytelling.

Neither Oakhurst nor his female companions cared to tell their personal experiences. So that plan would have failed, too, if not for the Innocent.

Some months before he had chanced upon a stray copy of Mr. Pope's clever translation of *The Iliad*.[9] The Innocent had thoroughly mastered the plot. However, he'd almost entirely forgotten the words. So now he proposed to narrate the main incidents of the poem in the **vernacular** of Sandy Bar.

For the rest of the night, the godlike heroes of Homer again walked the earth. Trojan bully and cunning Greek wrestled in the winds. The great pines in the canyon seemed to bow to the anger of the son of Peleus.

Mr. Oakhurst listened with quiet satisfaction. He was most especially interested in the fate of "Ash-heels." That was what the Innocent **persisted** in calling the "swift-footed Achilles."

So, with little food and much of Homer and the accordion, a week passed over the heads of the outcasts. The sun again left them. And again snowflakes sifted over the land from iron-gray skies.

Day by day the snowy circle drew closer around them. At last they looked from their prison over walls of dazzling

---

[9]Alexander Pope (1688-1744), an English poet, translated *The Iliad*. *The Iliad* is an ancient Greek epic poem said to have been written by a man called Homer. The poem tells of a war between Greeks and Trojans. Achilles, the son of Peleus, was the mightiest Greek warrior.

white drifts. The snow now towered twenty feet over their heads.

It became more and more difficult to get fuel for the fires. Even the fallen trees beside them were now half hidden in the drifts.

Yet no one complained. The lovers turned from the dreary sight and looked into each other's eyes. And then they were happy.

Mr. Oakhurst coolly settled down to play the losing game before him.

The Duchess was more cheerful than she had been. She assumed the care of Piney.

Only Mother Shipton seemed to sicken and fade. This despite the fact that she was once the strongest of the party.

At midnight on the tenth day, she called Oakhurst to her side.

"I'm going," she said in an irritable, weak voice. "But don't say anything about it. Don't waken the kids. Take the bundle from under my head and open it."

Mr. Oakhurst did so. It contained Mother Shipton's **rations** for the last week, untouched.

"Give 'em to the child," she said, pointing to the sleeping Piney.

"You've starved yourself," said the gambler.

"That's what they call it," said the woman snappishly as she lay down again. She turned her face to the wall and passed quietly away.

The accordion and the bones were put aside that day. Homer was forgotten, too.

When the body of Mother Shipton had been buried beneath the snow, Mr. Oakhurst took the Innocent aside. He showed Tom a pair of snowshoes. He'd made them from an old packsaddle.

"There's one chance in a hundred to save her yet," he said, pointing to Piney. "But it's there," he added, pointing toward Poker Flat. "If you can reach there in two days, she's safe."

"And you?" asked Tom Simson.

"I'll stay here," was the brief reply.

The lovers parted with a long embrace.

"You are not going, too?" said the Duchess. She saw that Mr. Oakhurst was apparently waiting to accompany Tom.

"As far as the canyon," he replied.

He turned suddenly and kissed the Duchess. The gesture left her pale face aflame and her trembling limbs **rigid** with amazement.

Night came but not Mr. Oakhurst. It brought the storm again and the whirling snow.

The Duchess went to feed the fire. She found that someone had quietly piled beside the hut enough fuel for a few more days. The tears rose to her eyes, but she hid them from Piney.

The women slept but little. In the morning they looked into each other's faces. There they read their fate. Neither spoke.

But Piney accepted the role of the stronger. She drew near and placed her arm around the Duchess' waist. They stayed like that for the rest of the day.

That night, the storm reached its greatest fury. It tore apart the protecting vines and invaded the hut.

Toward morning they found themselves unable to feed the fire. It had gradually died away. As the embers slowly blackened, the Duchess crept closer to Piney. She broke the silence of many hours.

"Piney, can you pray?"

"No, dear," said Piney simply.

The Duchess, without knowing exactly why, felt relieved. She put her head on Piney's shoulder and spoke no more. And so the young and purer supported the head of her soiled sister upon her virgin breast. In that position, they fell asleep.

The wind died down as if it feared to waken them. Feathery drifts of snow were shaken from the long pine branches. Like white winged birds, the drifts flew and then settled about the sleeping women.

Through the torn clouds, the moon looked down upon what had been the camp. But all human stain, all traces of earthly pain, were hidden. The spotless blanket mercifully flung from above covered it all.

They slept all that day and the next. Nor did they waken when voices and footsteps broke the silence of the camp.

Pitying fingers brushed the snow from the pale, weary faces. But you could scarcely have told which was the sinner. There was equal peace upon both faces.

Even the law of Poker Flat recognized this. The men turned away, leaving the two women with their arms still around one another.

But in the gulch on a large pine tree they found the two of clubs.[10] It had been pinned to the bark with a knife. It had this message on it, written in pencil with a firm hand.

BENEATH THIS TREE
LIES THE BODY
OF
JOHN OAKHURST.
HE STRUCK A STREAK OF BAD LUCK
ON NOVEMBER 23, 1850,
AND
HANDED IN HIS CHECKS
ON DECEMBER 7, 1850.

They found him pulseless and cold. There was a derringer[11] by his side and a bullet in his heart. But he was still as calm as in life. Beneath the snow he lay, both the strongest and yet the weakest of the outcasts of Poker Flat.

[10]The two of clubs is the lowest card in a deck.
[11]A derringer is a small pistol.

"The Outcasts of Poker Flat" was first published in 1869.

INSIGHTS INTO
BRET HARTE

(1836-1902)

At his peak, Harte was one of the most popular writers in the world. He once used that fame to get a cabin when a ship was booked up. (Rooms were often saved for such last-minute arrivals of the famous.)

A big, tough miner overheard Harte get the cabin he had just been refused. Scared by the glaring miner, Harte spent the next half hour trying to hide.

But Harte was finally cornered. The miner asked if he was Bret Harte, author of "The Luck of Roaring Camp."

Harte fearfully said he was.

The miner then swore, delighted. He demanded: "Put it there!" He had only wanted to shake the famous author's hand.

Harte once wrote a poem called "Plain Language for Truthful James." Under the nickname "The Heathen Chinee," the poem was an amazing hit. Thousands of magazines and newspapers reprinted it. Hotels, stores, and streetcars displayed copies. It was even sung.

Yet the poem was just an "accident," according to Harte. Simply to fill a gap in the newspaper where he worked, Harte added the poem. But first he had to dig it out of the wastebasket where he had tossed it earlier.

Harte had trouble writing anything unless he was broke. He even preferred to borrow funds—which he never repaid.

The *Atlantic Monthly,* a highly respected magazine, offered Harte $10,000 for a year's work. In those days, that sum was unbelievably high.

continued

Harte happily took and spent the money. But he did not even supply the twelve stories the magazine asked for on time. The *Atlantic Monthly* did not make the offer again.

Stories of the California gold rush made Harte famous as a writer. He continued to write tales about the gold rush, but left the state for good in 1871. Then he went to Europe in 1878. He actually spent the rest of his life there (twenty-four years). Not only did Harte desert his country, but also his wife and three children.

Other works by Harte:
"An Ingenue of the Sierras," short story
"The Luck of Roaring Camp," short story
"M'liss," short story
"Tennessee's Partner," short story

THE MAN WITHOUT A COUNTRY

EDWARD EVERETT HALE

VOCABULARY PREVIEW

Below is a list of words that appear in the story. Read the list and get to know the words before you start the story.

accumulated—gathered; stored up

adjourned—broke up a meeting; recessed

allusion—reference

chaos—total confusion or disorder

condense—make smaller or sum up

custody—imprisonment or "safekeeping" (as in custody of a child)

destined—fated; doomed

expedition—a journey for a special purpose

farce—mockery; joke

fervent—burning; passionate

hinder—block or restrain

libel—a statement or picture that unfairly damages a person's reputation

precautions—actions taken to avoid risk; safeguards

prosecution—legal actions taken against a person or group for a crime

prosperity—success and well-being

quaint—pleasantly old-fashioned and odd

rendezvous—a prearranged meeting or meeting place

sentimentalism—the quality of being overly emotional

shrine—a holy place, often containing sacred objects

spectacle—big public display or show

THE MAN
WITHOUT
A COUNTRY

EDWARD EVERETT HALE

Youthful pride tempts Philip Nolan into a foolish crime. That same pride then leads him to suggest his own dreadful sentence.

No, not iron bars, bread and water, or dark dungeons for Nolan. His torture is to be a man forever without a country.

I suppose very few readers of the *New York Herald* of August 13 observed the announcement. It was in an out-of-the-way corner among the "Deaths."

> NOLAN. Died, on board U.S. *Levant*,
> Lat. 2° 11' S., Long. 131° W., on May 11,
> PHILIP NOLAN.[1]

I happened to observe it because I was stranded at the old Mission House in Mackinaw. I was waiting for a Lake Superior steamer which did not choose to come.

---

[1] Lat. and long. are abbreviations for latitude and longitude, lines which show locations on a map. This information tells where Nolan's ship was when he died.

While waiting, I was devouring to the very last inch all the papers I could get hold of. I was even down to the death and marriage announcements in the *Herald*.

My memory for names and people is good. And, the reader will see, I had reason enough to remember Philip Nolan.

Hundreds of readers would have paused if the officer of the *Levant* had reported it differently. He might have written: "Died, May 11, THE MAN WITHOUT A COUNTRY."

That was the name that poor Philip Nolan had generally been called by the officers who had charge of him during some fifty years. Indeed, all the men who sailed with Nolan called him that.

There were many men who had wine with him once every two weeks during a three years' cruise. Yet I dare say they never knew his name was Nolan. Indeed, they may not have known the poor devil had any name at all.

There can now be no possible harm in telling this poor creature's story. But there had been reason enough until now. Strict secrecy prevented it.

In fact, keeping the secret had been a matter of honor among gentlemen of the Navy who took care of Nolan. It had been that way ever since President Madison left office in 1817.

It certainly speaks well for the loyalty and personal honor of navy men that this man's story has been unknown to the press. And, I think, it has been unknown to the country at large.

When I was stationed ashore, I looked into this case. And I believe that every report about Nolan was burned when Ross set fire to the public buildings in Washington.[2]

One of the Tuckers, or maybe one of the Watsons, was in charge of Nolan at the end of the war. When he returned from his cruise, he reported about Nolan to one of the

[2]Many public buildings in Washington were burned by the British during the War of 1812. General Robert Ross led this British attack.

Crowninshields in the Navy Department. He found that the Department ignored the whole business.

The Department may have really known nothing about Nolan. Or they may have just been pretending not to know about him. I'm not sure.

But this I do know. Since 1817, and possibly before, no naval officer has mentioned Nolan in a report.

But, as I said, there is no need for secrecy any longer. The poor creature is dead. And it seems worthwhile to tell a little of his story. By doing so, I hope to show today's young Americans what it is to be A MAN WITHOUT A COUNTRY.

Philip Nolan was one of the finest young officers in the Legion of the West. That was what the western forces of our army were called then.

Aaron Burr[3] met this dashing, bright young fellow in 1805. Burr was making his first **expedition** down to New Orleans at the time. I think they actually met at some dinner party.

Burr noticed Nolan and talked to him. Then he took Nolan on a two-day voyage in his flat boat. In short, he impressed Nolan.

The next year, army life was very dull for poor Nolan. He sometimes wrote to Burr, as the great man allowed him to do. The poor boy wrote and rewrote and copied long, awkward letters. But he never received a line in reply.

The other boys sneered at Nolan for wasting his time and admiration on a politician. Their time was better spent devoted to whiskey and cards. Bourbon and poker were still unknown.

But one day Nolan had his revenge. Burr came down the river again. But this time he did not come as a lawyer

[3]Aaron Burr (1756-1836) was vice-president of the U.S. from 1801-1805. He was accused of secretly trying to lead part of the U.S. to break from the rest of the country. Burr was tried for treason on this charge but found innocent.

seeking a place for his office. This time he came as a conqueror in disguise.

Burr had defeated I do not know how many district attorneys. He had dined at I do not know how many public dinners. He had been praised in I do not know how many weekly papers. And it was rumored that he had an army behind him and an empire before him.

His arrival marked a great day for poor Nolan. Burr had not been at the fort an hour before he sent for him.

That evening he asked Nolan to take him out in a boat. He said he wanted to see some of the sights on the great river. But Burr really intended to win Nolan to his cause.

By the time the sail was over, Nolan had signed up, body and soul. From that time—though he did not yet know—he lived as a man without a country.

I do not know what Burr meant to do, dear reader, any more than you. It is not our concern just now.

But then Jefferson and his party began trying anyone suspected of treason.

So to while away the boring summer, some of the lesser fry in the Mississippi Valley did the same. They set up one of their own **spectacles** on the little backwoods stage at Fort Adams. There they carried out a string of court-martials[4] on the officers.

One after another of the colonels and majors were tried for treason. And to fill out the list, they added poor little Nolan.

Heaven knows, there was enough evidence against him. He was sick of the service and had been willing to be disloyal. Plus, Nolan would have obeyed any order had it been signed, "By command of His Excellency, A. Burr."

The courts dragged on. The big flies escaped. This may have been fair for all I know. Yet Nolan was proved guilty enough, as I have said.

---

[4]Court-martials are military trials.

You and I would never have heard of him if he had not spoken at the close of the trial. The president of the court asked Nolan if he wished to say anything to show he had been faithful to the United States.

Nolan cried out, "D--n[5] the United States! I wish I may never hear of the United States again!"

I suppose he did not know how the words shocked old Colonel Morgan. (Morgan was in charge of the court.) Half the officers in the room had served during the Revolution. They had risked their lives for the very idea Nolan now so boldly cursed in his madness. They, too, were shocked by this brash young man.

For his part, Nolan had grown up in the part of the country known in those days as the West. He had been educated on a plantation. Their finest visitor was a Spanish officer or a French merchant from Orleans.

Nolan's education, such as it was, he gained on business trips to Vera Cruz. And I think he told me his father once hired an Englishman to tutor him one winter. He spent half his youth with an older brother hunting horses in Texas. So "United States" was scarcely a reality to him.

Yet he had been fed by "United States" for all his years in the army. He had sworn on his faith as a Christian to be true to "United States." It was "United States" which gave him the uniform and sword he wore.

Also, my poor Nolan, the "United States" had picked you as one of her loyal men of honor. That was the only reason Burr cared for you any more than for one of the common sailors on his boat.

I do not excuse Nolan. I only explain why he damned his country and wished never to hear her name again.

He never did hear her name but once again. From that moment (September 23, 1807) till the day he died (May 11, 1863) he never heard her name again. For over half of a century, he was a man without a country.

[5]Writers and editors of the past often blanked out words that might offend readers. Nolan is saying "damn."

Old Morgan, as I said, was terribly shocked. He could not have felt worse if Nolan had compared George Washington to Benedict Arnold or cried "God Save King George."

Morgan called the court into his private room. He returned in fifteen minutes with a face like a sheet.

He said to Nolan, "Prisoner, hear the sentence of the court! If the President approves, the court orders that you never hear the name of the United States again."

Nolan laughed. But nobody else laughed. Old Morgan was too solemn. The whole room was hushed dead as night for a minute. Even Nolan soon lost his swagger.

Then Morgan added, "Mr. Marshal, take the prisoner to Orleans in an armed boat. Deliver him to the naval commander there."

The Marshal gave his orders. Then the prisoner was taken out of the court.

"Mr. Marshal," continued old Morgan, "see that no one mentions the United States to the prisoner. Give my regards to Lieutenant Mitchell at Orleans. Have him order that no one shall mention the United States to the prisoner while he is aboard.

"You will receive your written orders from the officer on duty here this evening. The court is **adjourned** without delay."

I always assumed Colonel Morgan himself took the court records to Washington and explained them to Jefferson. It is certain the President approved them. That is, it is certain if I can believe the men who say they saw his signature.

Before the *Nautilus* reached the North Atlantic coast with the prisoner, the sentence had been approved. Nolan was a man without a country.

The plan used then was basically the same which was followed forever after. The Secretary of the Navy (perhaps the first Crowninshield) was to put Nolan on a government ship going on a long cruise.

Nolan was not actually to be locked up. The officers were only to make certain that he never saw or heard of the country.

We had few long cruises then. Also, the navy was very much out of favor. Therefore, I do not know for certain what his first cruise was. As I have said, most of this story had been handed down.

It may have been Tingey or Shaw who first had charge of Nolan. However, I think it was one of the younger men. (We are all old enough now!)

At any rate, the first commander arranged the rules and **precautions** of the affair. His rules were followed, I suppose, till Nolan died.

Thirty years after, when I was second officer of the *Intrepid,* I saw the original written orders. I have been sorry ever since that I did not copy it all.

However, it ran something like this.

Washington [the date must
have been late in 1807]

Sir:

You will receive from Lieutenant Neale a man named Philip Nolan. He was lately a lieutenant in the United States Army.

This person, at his court-martial, said that he wished he might "never hear of the United States again."

The Court sentenced him to have his wish come true.

For now, the President has given this department the power to carry out this order.

You will take the prisoner on board your ship. Keep him there with such precautions that will prevent his escape.

You will provide him with room, food, and clothes proper for an officer of his former rank. Treat him as if he were a lieutenant on the business of his government.

The gentlemen on board can decide their own relationships with him. He is not to suffer any insults of any kind. Nor is he ever to be needlessly reminded that he is a prisoner.

But for no reason is he ever to hear of his country or see any information about it. You are to caution all officers under your command. Tell them that any other freedoms may be granted. But this rule, which involves his punishment, shall not be broken.

The government wishes that he shall never again see the country which he rejected. Before the end of your cruise, you will receive orders to this effect.

> Respectfully yours,
> W. SOUTHARD, for the
> Secretary of the Navy

If I had only copied the whole letter, there would have been no break in my story. For Captain Shaw (if it was he) handed it to the next commander. That person handed it down again.

I suppose the commander of the *Levant* has it today. It gives him the authority for keeping this man in **custody**.

The rule adopted on ships where I met "the man without a country" was handed down from the first, I think. No mess[6] liked to eat with him very often. His presence cut off all talk of home or of going back to the U.S.

No one could talk about politics or letters or peace or war, either. Nolan cut off more than half the talk men liked to have at sea.

But it was always thought too cruel that he should never meet the rest of us, except to tip our hats. So we finally sank into one system.

[6]A mess is a group of people who dine together.

Nolan was not permitted to talk with the men unless an officer was nearby. With officers, he could talk as much as he and they chose. But he grew shy, though he had favorites. I was one.

The captain always asked him to dinner on Monday. Every mess after that invited him in turn. The size of the ship determined how often he appeared at your mess.

He ate his breakfast in his stateroom—he always had a stateroom. A guard or somebody could watch his door there. And whatever else he ate or drank, he ate or drank alone.

Sometimes when the sailors had a special party, they were allowed to invite "Plain Buttons." (That was what they called him.) Nolan was then sent with an officer, and the men were forbidden to speak of home while he was there. I believe the theory was that the sight of his punishment was good for them.

They called him Plain Buttons because of his clothes. Nolan always chose to wear a standard army uniform. However, he was not permitted to wear the army button. That's because the button would have shown either the initials or the symbol of the country he had rejected.

I remember, soon after I joined the navy, I was on shore with some of the older officers from our ship. Some officers from the *Brandywine* were also there. We had met that ship at Alexandria in Egypt.

We were allowed to get a group together and go up to Cairo and the pyramids. We jogged along on donkeys (that is how you went then). Some of the gentlemen began talking about Nolan.

Someone told about the system for Nolan's books and other reading. Nolan was almost never permitted to go on shore. He wasn't even allowed out if the ship was in port for months. So his time hung heavy.

Everyone was permitted to lend him books. But the books could not be published in America or make any **allusion** to it.

This kind of book was common enough in the old days. At that time other countries spoke as little about the United States as we do of Paraguay.

Sooner or later, Nolan read almost all the foreign papers aboard ship. But before he could read them, somebody had to go over them. Any ad or stray paragraph that alluded to America had to be cut out.

This was a little cruel sometimes. The back of what was cut out might be totally innocent. Right in the midst of one of Napoleon's battles or Canning's speeches,[7] poor Nolan would find a great hole. The cut had been made because of an ad for a boat to New York or a message from the President on the back.

As I said, that was the first time I had heard of this plan. Afterwards, I had more than enough to do with it.

I remember the talk because of what Phillips said. As soon as Nolan's reading was alluded to, Phillips told a story. The tale concerned something that happened at the Cape of Good Hope on Nolan's first voyage. It is the only thing I ever knew of that voyage.

They had docked at the Cape. They also had exchanged greetings with the English Admiral and his fleet.

They were leaving for a long cruise up the Indian Ocean. So Phillips borrowed a lot of books from an English officer. In those days (even now), that was quite a windfall.

Among the books—as ill luck would have it—was the *Lay of the Last Minstrel*.[8] They had all heard of this book. However, most of them had not seen it. I think it had just been published.

Well, nobody thought there could be anything national in that. Phillips did swear, though, that old Shaw had cut out *The Tempest* from Shakespeare before giving it to

---

[7]Napoleon (1769-1821) was a French conqueror of Europe. George Canning (1770-1827) was a British foreign minister during Napoleon's time.

[8]This poem is by Scottish novelist and poet Sir Walter Scott (1771-1832). A lay is a poem meant to be sung.

Nolan. Shaw said, "The Bermudas ought to be ours. And by heaven, they shall be one day."

So one afternoon a lot of the men sat on deck smoking and reading aloud. People do not do such things now, it seems. But when I was young, we got rid of a great deal of time that way. And Nolan was permitted to join the circle.

Well, it so happened that Nolan took the book and read to the others. He read very well, as I know.

Nobody in the circle knew a line of the poem. They only knew it was all about magic and knights and events that happened ten thousand years ago.

Poor Nolan read steadily through the fifth section. He stopped a minute and drank something. Then he began again, without a thought of what was coming.

> Breathes there the man, with soul so dead,
> Who never to himself has said,—

It seems impossible to us that anybody ever heard this familiar line for the first time. But that was the case with all these fellows. And poor Nolan went on, still unaware.

> This is my own, my native land!

Then they all realized what was about to happen. But Nolan expected to get through it. I suppose he turned a little pale. He then plunged on.

> Whose heart has never within him burned,
> As home his footsteps he has turned
>   From wandering on foreign sand?—
> If such a man breathes, go, note him well.

By this time the men were all beside themselves. They wished there was a way to make him skip two pages.

But Nolan was too confused for that. He coughed a little; his face turned bright red. Then he staggered on.

> For him no glorious songs swell.
> His titles may be high, his name proud,
> His wealth as great as could be wished.
> Despite these titles, power, and wealth,
> The wretch concentrated all on himself—

Here the poor fellow choked. He could not go on. Instead, he jumped up and flung the book into sea. Then he vanished into his stateroom.

"By heaven," said Phillips, "we did not see him again for two months. And I had to make up a story to tell that English doctor why I did not return his book."

That story shows about when Nolan's hollow courage must have broken down. They said that at first he took a very proud tone. He seemed to consider his imprisonment a mere **farce**. He pretended to enjoy the voyage and all that.

But Phillips said that after he came out of his stateroom, he never was the same man. He rarely read aloud again. He would only touch the Bible or Shakespeare or something else he knew.

But it was not only his reading that changed. He was never exactly a friend again to the young men. From that day forward, he was always shy.

When I knew him, he seldom spoke unless he was spoken to. Only with a very few friends was it different. Then he would sometimes show a little spirit when he talked. But generally he had the nervous, tired look of a heart-wounded man.

Another event occurred as Captain Shaw (if it was Shaw, as I said) was coming home. He made a surprise stop on one of the Windward Islands, off South America. The boys said the officers were sick of salted meat. They meant to have turtle soup before they came home.

After several days, the *Warren* came to the same **rendez-vous**. The two ships exchanged signals.

The *Warren* sent to Phillips and these homeward-bound men letters and papers. She told them she was outward bound, perhaps to the Mediterranean. Then she took poor Nolan and his gear on board to try his second cruise.

Nolan looked very blank when he was told to get ready to join his new ship. He had known from watching the sky that until that moment he was going "home."

But this turn of events showed him something he may not have thought of. It showed that there was no going home for him, even to prison.

This was the first of some twenty such transfers. Sooner or later, he had been aboard half our best vessels. But they always kept him some hundred miles from the country he had hoped he might never see again.

It may have been on that second cruise that Mrs. Graff danced with him. Mrs. Graff was a famous southern beauty of those days.

The ship had been docked a long time in the Bay of Naples.[9] The officers were very close to some men in the English fleet, and there had been many parties. So the men thought they must give a great ball on board the ship.

How they ever did it on board the *Warren* I am sure I do not know. Perhaps it was not the *Warren*. Or perhaps ladies did not take up as much room as they do now.

They wanted to use Nolan's stateroom for something. They hated to do that without asking him to the ball. So the captain said they could ask him. He only ordered that they be sure he did not talk with people who would give him information.

[9]The Bay of Naples lies to the southwest of Italy.

So the dance went on. It was the finest party that had ever been known, I dare say. (I have never heard of a ball on a warship that was not.)

The ladies present were the family of the American ambassador and one or two travelers. A group of English girls and mothers also came. Perhaps Lady Hamilton herself was there.

Well, different officers took turns talking with Nolan in a friendly way. They were trying to make sure that nobody else spoke to him.

The dancing went on in high spirits. After a while, even those who guarded Nolan ceased to fear anything would occur. Only when an English lady called for American dances did an odd thing happen.

Everyone at that time danced folk dances. The black band did some talking before they decided what American dances were. Then they willingly started off with "Virginia Reel." They followed that with "Money Musk."

In those days, it should have been followed in turn by "The Old Thirteen." Dick, the leader, tapped for the fiddles to begin. He bent forward about to say, " 'The Old Thirteen,' gentleman and ladies!" But just then the captain's boy tapped him on the shoulder and whispered something.

So Dick did not announce the name of the dance. He merely bowed, began the tune, and they all danced. The officers taught the English girls the steps. However, they did not tell them why it had no name.

But that is not the story I started to tell. As the dancing went on, Nolan and our fellows became more at ease, as I said. In fact, it next seemed quite natural for him to bow to the splendid Mrs. Graff.

Smiling, he said, "I hope you have not forgotten me, Miss Rutledge. Shall I have the honor of a dance?"

He did it so quickly that Fellows, who was by him, could not **hinder** him.

She laughed and said, "I am not Miss Rutledge any longer, Mr. Nolan. But I will dance all the same."

She nodded to Fellows as if to say he must leave Nolan to her. Then she led Nolan off to the dance floor.

Nolan thought he had his chance. He had known her in Philadelphia. He had met her at other places, as well. This was a blessing from heaven.

You could not talk while doing folk dances as you could with slower steps. But there were chances for voices and sounds, for eyes and blushes.

Nolan began by asking Mrs. Graff about her travels. He questioned her about Europe and Mt. Vesuvius and the French.

Finally they had worked through it all. Yet that long talking time at the end of a dance set remained.

As Mrs. Graff told me years later, Nolan turned a little pale at this point. But he asked boldly, "And what do you hear from home, Mrs. Graff?"

That splendid creature looked right through him. Heavens! How she must have looked through him!

"Home!! Mr. Nolan!! I thought you were the man who never wanted to hear of home again!!"

Then she walked directly up the deck to her husband. She left poor Nolan alone, as he always was. He did not dance again.

I cannot give any history of this man in order. Nobody can now. Indeed, I'm not trying to. These are stories which have been passed down. I sort them out from the myths that have been told about him for forty years.

A great many lies have been told about Nolan. The fellows used to say he was the Iron Mask.[10]

---

[10]The Iron Mask was a mysterious French prisoner. He was jailed from 1698 until his death in 1703. His identity was kept a secret by the fact that he was forced to wear a mask.

And George Pons went to his grave believing Nolan wrote *Junius*.[11] Pons thought that Nolan was being punished for this **libel** on Thomas Jefferson. Obviously, Pons was not very strong in his history.

A happier story than either of those I have told concerns the War.[12] That came along soon after. I have heard this story told in three or four ways. Indeed, it may have happened more than once. But which ship it was on I cannot tell.

The incident occurred during one of those great sea battles with the English. It happened that enemy fire hit a part of the ship. The shot took out the officer and men in charge of the cannon.

Now you can say what you choose about courage. But that is not a nice thing to see.

The men who were not killed picked themselves up. As they were helping the doctor carry off the bodies, Nolan appeared. He was in shirt sleeves and held the rammer[13] in his hand.

He gave them orders just as if he had been the officer. His directions were given with complete authority. He announced who should go with the wounded men and who should stay with him.

His voice was perfectly cheery. He used that tone which makes men feel things will be all right. And he finished loading the gun with his own hands. Then he aimed it and told the men to fire.

There he stayed, captain of that gun. He kept those fellows in good spirits till the enemy struck. He sat on the cannon

[11]The Junius letters appeared in a London newspaper from 1769 to 1772. The author, who was not known, criticized King George III and his ministers (not Jefferson).

[12]The War of 1812 (which lasted until 1814) was between the U.S. and Britain. The war was partly caused because the English forced some American sailors to serve in the British navy.

[13]A rammer is a long pole with a block of wood at the end. It is used to force shot down into a cannon.

while it cooled. And all that time, he was exposed to enemy fire.

Nolan showed them easier ways to handle the heavy shot, too. He made the new hands laugh at their own blunders. And when the gun cooled again, he got it loaded. He actually had them firing twice as often as any other gun on the ship.

The captain came around to encourage the men. Nolan tipped his hat and said, "I am showing them how a weapons expert would do it, sir."

And this is the part of the story where all the legends agree. The Commodore said, "I see you do, and I thank you, sir. I shall never forget this day and neither shall you."

After this whole thing was over, the Commodore stood on deck. The Englishman's sword was in his hand.[14]

He said, "Where is Mr. Nolan? Ask Mr. Nolan to come here."

When Nolan came, the captain said, "Mr. Nolan, we are all very grateful to you. You are one of us today. You will be mentioned in the reports."

And then the old man took off his own sword. He gave it to Nolan and made him put it on. The man told me this who saw it.

Nolan cried like a baby. And who could blame the man? He had not worn a sword since that horrid day in Fort Adams. But always afterward, on special occasions, Nolan wore that **quaint**, old sword of the Commodore's.

The captain did mention him in the reports. It was always said he asked that Nolan might be pardoned. He wrote a special letter to the Secretary of War.

But nothing ever came of it. As I said, that was about the time they began to ignore the whole affair in Washington. Nolan's imprisonment continued because nobody would stop it without new orders.

[14]By custom, a leader who lost a fight would surrender his sword to the winner.

I have heard it said that Nolan was with Porter when he took Nuku Hiva. Not the young Porter, you know. I mean old David Porter, his father.[15]

As I have said, Nolan had been an army officer. And he had served in the West. As a result, he knew more about how a solid fort was built than any of them did. And he fixed the guns with a hearty good will.

I have always thought it was a pity Porter did not leave Nolan in command there. That would have settled all the question about his punishment.

In turn, we would have kept the islands. At this moment we would have a station in the Pacific Ocean. And when the French wanted this little watering-place, they would have found it occupied. But, of course, James Madison and his party flung all that away.

That was nearly fifty years ago. If Nolan was thirty, then he must have been near eighty when he died. He looked sixty when he was forty. But he never seemed to me to change a hair afterwards.

I have imagined his life from what I have seen and heard. And I believe he must have been in every sea. Yet I think he was almost never on land.

He also must have known more officers in our service than any man alive.

He told me once, with a grave smile, that no man in the world lived a life as orderly as he. "You know the boys say I am the Iron Mask. And you know how busy he was."

He said it was not good for anyone to try to read all the time. After all, no one should do any one task all the time. He read just five hours a day.

"Then," he said, "I keep up my notebooks. I write in them at certain hours about my reading. Part of that time is also spent on my scrapbooks."

These scrapbooks were very curious indeed. He had six or eight of them on different subjects. There was one of

[15]Nuku Hiva is one of the Marquesas Islands in the Pacific. David Porter was a captain of a warship that sailed the Pacific.

History and one of Natural Science. There was even one which he called "Odds and Ends."

They were not merely books of newspaper clippings. They had bits of plants and ribbons, shells, and carved scraps of bone and wood.

The books were beautifully illustrated. Nolan drew quite well. He had some of the funniest drawings I have ever seen. But there were some very touching ones, too. I wonder who will have Nolan's scrapbooks.

Nolan said his reading and his notes were his work. He devoted five hours to the reading and two hours to his notes.

"Then," he said, "every man should have a pastime as well as work. Natural history is my pastime." That took two more hours a day.

The men used to bring him birds and fish. On a long cruise, he had to settle for centipedes and cockroaches. He was the only naturalist I ever met who knew the habits of the fly and mosquito.

All those naturalists can tell you what type the insects were. But ask them how to get rid of them. Or ask how they get away when you swat at them. About these matters the experts know as little as an idiot does.

These nine hours made up Nolan's regular "work." The rest of the time he talked or walked. He kept up his exercise until he grew very old.

And I never heard that he was ill. If any other man was ill, he was the kindest nurse in the world. He knew more than half of what the doctors did.

Then if anybody was sick or died, or if the captain requested, he was always ready to read prayers. I have said that he read beautifully.

I met Philip Nolan six or eight years after the War. It was on my first voyage after I was made a midshipman.[16]

---

[16]A midshipman is a student who is training to become a naval officer.

It was in the days after our Slave Trade treaty had been signed.[17] The party in power still felt some **sentimentalism** about the issue. They believed that the horrors of the slave trade should be stamped out.

So something was sometimes done to satisfy them. We were in the South Atlantic on that business.

From the time I joined, I believe I thought Nolan was a sort of chaplain (in a blue coat). I never asked about him. Everything in the ship was strange to me. I knew I would look like a greenhorn to ask questions. I suppose I thought there was a Plain Buttons on every ship.

Nolan dined with our mess once a week. We were warned on that day not to say anything about home.

But they could have told us not to say anything about Mars or a book of the Bible. I still would not have asked why. There were a great many things which seemed to me to have as little reason.

One day we caught up with a dirty little ship. There were slaves on board. That event first opened my eyes to the history of the man without a country.

An officer was sent to take charge of the little ship. After a few minutes, he sent his boat back. He wanted to know if any of us spoke Portuguese.

We all wished we could when the captain asked us. But not any of the the officers did.

The captain was starting to move on and ask other shipmen. Just then Nolan stepped forward. He said he would be glad to interpret if the captain wished.

The captain thanked him and got another boat ready for him. It was in this boat that I was lucky enough to go.

When we got there, it was a scene such as you seldom see and never want to. The nastiness and **chaos** were beyond description.

[17]A slave trade treaty was passed in 1807. This treaty ordered that no more slaves be shipped to America. After the treaty was passed, American ships sometimes stopped slaving vessels and freed slaves.

There were not a great many of the black men. But in order to make them understand they were free, Vaughan had their chains removed. He then began to put the chains on the ship's crew.

Most of the blacks were out of the hold. They were now swarming all around the dirty deck. A bunch of them surrounded Vaughan. They were addressing him in every kind of language.

As we came on deck, Vaughan looked down from the top of a barrel where he stood. He cried, "For God's love, is there anybody who can make these people understand?

"The men gave them rum. But that did not quiet them.

"Then I knocked that big fellow down twice. But that didn't soothe him.

"And I said something in Indian language to all of them. Believe it or not, they understood that as well as English."

Nolan said he could speak Portuguese. One or two handsome blacks from Liberia were dragged forward. It had already been discovered that they had worked for the Portuguese.

"Tell them they are free," said Vaughan. "And tell them that these rascals will be hanged as soon as we can get enough rope."

Nolan explained it in a way the two blacks could understand. In turn, they explained it to those who could understand them.

Yells of delight, clenching of fists, leaping, and dancing followed. Some even kissed Nolan's feet. Many rushed to worship Vaughan as the one who had brought it all about.

Vaughan was pleased. "Tell them," he said, "that I will take them all to Cape Palmas."[18]

This was not received as well. Cape Palmas was a long way from most of their homes. They would be forever separated from their homes if they were taken to Cape Palmas.

[18]Cape Palmas is a port in West Africa.

Their interpreters instantly said, "Ah, no Palmas." Then they began to suggest other solutions in loud voices.

Vaughan was rather disappointed they were not pleased by his generosity. He eagerly asked Nolan what they said.

Drops of sweat stood on poor Nolan's white forehead as he hushed the men. He said, "He says, 'Not Palmas.' He says, 'Take us home, take us to our own country. Take us to our own house, our own children, our own women.' He says he has an old father and mother who will die if they do not see him.

"And this one says he left his people all sick. He paddled down to the city to beg the white doctor for help. That is when these devils caught him and took him away. He has never seen anybody from home since then.

"And this one says," Nolan choked out, "that he has not heard a word from his home in six months. Not a word while he has been locked up in their hellish jail."

Vaughan always said he grew gray himself while Nolan struggled to speak for the men. I did not understand the passion involved. But even I saw that the air was melting with **fervent** heat. Something was going to have to break somewhere.

The Negroes noticed it, too, and stopped howling. They saw Nolan's agony and Vaughan's almost equal agony of sympathy.

As quick as Vaughan could speak, he said, "Tell them yes, yes, yes. Tell them they shall go to the Mountains of the Moon, if they wish. Even if I have to sail through the Great White Desert, they shall go home!"[19]

Nolan translated the speech in so many words. And then they all tried to kiss him again and rub his nose with theirs.

But Nolan could not stand it long. With permission from Vaughan, he got back into our boat.

He beckoned me to sit with him. As we set sail, he said to me, "Youngster, let that be a lesson. Let it show you

[19]The mountains are in east central Africa. The Great White Desert is probably the Sahara in northern Africa.

what it is to be without a family, without a home, and without a country.

"Think about it if you are ever tempted to say or do something that will distance you from your family, home, or country. Pray God to take you that instant to His heaven.

"Stick by your family, boy. Forget you have a self. Do everything for them. Think of your home, boy. Write letters and talk about it. Let it be nearer and nearer to your thoughts the farther you have to travel from it.

"Then rush back to it when you are free. Do as that poor black slave is doing now."

The words began to rattle in his throat. "And for your country, boy, and for that flag," he pointed to the ship, "never dream a dream but of serving her. Serve her as she asks you. Serve her even if you must go through a thousand hells.

"No matter what happens to you—who flatters or hurts you—never look at another flag. Never let a night pass but you pray God to bless that flag.

"Remember, boy. Behind all these men—behind officers, government, even people—there is the Country Herself. Your Country. You belong to Her as you belong to your own mother.

"Stand by Her, boy. Defend her as you would your mother if those devils there had got hold of her today!"

I was frightened to death by his calm, hard passion. But somehow I stammered that I would do what he said, by all that was holy. I added that I had never thought of doing anything else.

He hardly seemed to hear me. But he did add, almost in a whisper, "Oh, if anybody had said that to me when I was your age!"

I have never told this story till now. I think we became great friends because of that talk we had.

He was certainly very kind to me. He often stayed up to walk the decks with me during my night duty. He explained a great deal of math to me. In fact, it is because of him that I like math. He loaned me books and helped me with my reading.

He never alluded to his story again. But over thirty years, I have learned from one officer or another what I am telling.

We parted from him in St. Thomas harbor, at the end of our cruise. I was more sorry than I can say.

I was very glad to meet Nolan again in 1830. Then, later in life, I tried to move heaven and earth to have him released. I thought I had some influence in Washington by that time.

But it was like getting a ghost out of prison. They pretended there is no such man. Never was such a man. They will say this at the Department even now!

Perhaps they do not know. It will not be the first incident which the Department appears to know nothing about!

There is a story that Nolan met Burr once on one of our ships. But this I believe to be a lie. Or maybe it is a myth which rings true but is not.

The story tells of a tremendous blowup between Nolan and Burr. Nolan taunted Burr by asking him how *he* liked being "without a country."

But it is clear from Burr's life that this could not have happened. I mention this only to show the rumors that crop up around a mysterious man like Nolan.

So poor Philip Nolan had his wish fulfilled. I know only one fate more dreadful. It is the fate of those who will have to leave their country because they tried to ruin her. At the same time, they shall watch her **prosperity** and honor rise once rid of their wickedness.

Poor Nolan's wish was the same wish of every soldier and sailor who broke their oath two years ago.[20] (We called Nolan poor not because his punishment was too great. No, we called him that because he so clearly repented.)

[20]The narrator is referring to Southerners who deserted the U.S. during the Civil War.

I do not know how often the outcasts have repented their actions. I do know they have done all they could to separate themselves from their country. They have scattered all honors, bonds, memories, and hopes which belong to country. They have torn these ties into little shreds and thrown them to the wind.

I know, too, what pain they will go through. They will live what is left of their lives in foreign towns. And they are **destined** to blame each other till they die. The fate of these men will be as painful as Nolan's punishment.

Added to that, everyone who sees them will hate and curse them. Yes, they will have their wish, like Nolan.

As for poor Nolan, he repented his foolish actions. Then, like a man, he accepted the fate he had asked for. He never made the duty of his jailors more difficult or awkward. Accidents would happen. But they were never his fault.

Lieutenant Truxton told me about a discussion that occurred when Texas became a state. The officers debated whether they should cut Texas out of Nolan's handsome maps.

Nolan had two maps, one of the world and one of Mexico. The United States had been cut out when the atlas was bought for him.

But it was voted, rightly enough, that this would reveal to him what had happened. Or, as Harry Cole said, would make Nolan think Old Burr had succeeded.

So it was no fault of Nolan's that a great botch happened at my own mess table.

For a short time, I was in command of the *George Washington*. We were stationed in South America, anchored in the La Plata. Some officers who had been on shore had just joined us again. They were entertaining us with tales of their adventures riding half-wild horses.

Nolan was at our table. He was in an unusually bright, talkative mood. One of their stories reminded him of an adventure when he was catching wild horses in Texas with his brother Stephen. He must have been just a boy at the time.

He told the story with a good deal of spirit. In fact, the silence which follows a good story hung over the table after he had finished.

Then Nolan broke the silence himself. He asked, quite unaware of what he was saying, "What has become of Texas?

"After the Mexicans got their independence, I thought Texas would progress very fast. It is really one of the finest regions on earth. But I have not seen or heard a word of Texas for nearly twenty years."

There were two Texan officers at the table. There was good reason he had never heard of Texas. All information about it had been cut out of his newspapers since large numbers of Americans began settling there. While he could read of other countries, he could not read of Texas. So this region where his brother had traveled and died had ceased to exist for him.

Waters and Williams, the two Texans, looked at each other and tried not to laugh. Edward Morris stared at the captain's chandelier. Watrous was seized with a sneezing fit.

Nolan himself saw something was up, though he did not know what. And I, as host of the feast, had to speak.

"Texas is out of the map, Mr. Nolan. Have you seen Captain Back's curious account of Sir Thomas Roe's Welcome?"

After that cruise, I never saw Nolan again. I wrote to him at least twice a year. During that voyage we became even closer friends. But he never wrote to me.

The other men tell me that in those fifteen years he aged very fast. That might well be expected. But he was still the same gentle, silent sufferer that he ever was. He continued to bear as best he could the sentence he had set for himself.

Perhaps he was less social with the men he did not know. But he was more anxious than ever to serve and teach the boys. Some of those boys almost worshipped him.

And now, it seems the dear old fellow is dead. He has found a home at last, and a country.

Earlier, I had wondered if I should print this story. I had wanted to warn the young Nolans of today what it means to throw away a country.

But since writing this, I received a letter from Danforth. He is on board the *Levant*. The letter gives an account of Nolan's last hours. It has removed all my doubts.

To understand the letter, the reader should remember what happened after 1817. Since that date, every officer in charge of Nolan was in a delicate position. The government had failed to renew the original 1807 order regarding him.

What was a man to do? Should he let him go? If he did, would he then be charged for disobeying the order of 1807?

Should he keep him? But then what if Nolan should be freed someday? Suppose he sued them for illegal imprisonment or kidnapping?

I urged and stressed this to Southard. I have reason to think other officers did the same thing.

But the Secretary always said—as they often do in Washington—there were no special orders. He said that we must act on our own judgment.

That means, "If you succeed, you will be supported. If you fail, you will be criticized."

Well, all that is over now as Danforth says. I may risk **prosecution** simply for telling this story.

Here is the letter.

LEVANT, 2° 2' S.@ 131° W.

Dear Fred,

I try to find heart and life to tell you that all is over with dear old Nolan. I have been with him on this voyage more than I ever was. Now I understand why you used to speak of the dear old fellow as you did.

I could see he was not strong. But I had no idea the end was so near. The doctor had been watching him very carefully.

Yesterday morning the doctor told me Nolan was not very well. He had not even left his stateroom. I never recall this happening before.

He had let the doctor come and see him as he lay there. That was the first time the doctor had been in the stateroom. And he asked to see me.

Oh dear! Do you remember the mysteries we invented about his room in the old *Intrepid* days?

Well, I went in. There the poor fellow lay in his bed. He smiled pleasantly as he offered me his hand. Yet he looked very weak and frail.

I could not help glancing around his room. I saw that he had made a little **shrine** of his bunk. Stars and stripes were fixed above and around a picture of Washington. And he had painted a majestic eagle. One foot clutched the whole globe, which his wings overshadowed.

The dear old boy saw my glance. He said, with a sad smile, "Here, you see, I have a country!"

And then he pointed to the foot of the bed. I noticed there for the first time a great map of the United States. He had drawn it from memory and put it there to look at as he lay.

Quaint, old names were on it in large letters. "Indiana Territory," "Mississippi Territory," and "Louisiana Territory" were some of the labels.

The old fellow had patched in Texas, too. His western boundary reached all the way to the Pacific. But on that shore he had defined nothing.

"Oh, Danforth," he said, "I know I am dying. I cannot get home. Surely you will tell me something now?

"Stop! Stop! Do not speak until I say what I am sure

you know. There is no man on this ship, nor in America, as loyal as I. There cannot be a man who loves the old flag as I do. Nor can there be anyone who prays for it as I do.

"There are thirty-four stars in it now, Danforth. I do not know what their names are. Yet I thank God they are there.

"There has never been one taken away. I thank God for that, too. It means there has never been any successful Burr.

"Oh, Danforth, Danforth," he sighed. "A boy's idea of fame and freedom seems like a nightmare when one looks back on it after such a life as mine.

"But tell me—tell me something. Tell me everything, Danforth, before I die!"

Ingham, I swear I felt like a monster for not having told him everything before. Danger or no danger, delicacy or no delicacy. Who was I to act like a dictator over this dear, sainted, old man? He had made up for the madness of a boy's treason years ago.

"Mr. Nolan," I said, "I will tell you everything you ask. Only, where shall I begin?"

Oh, the blessed smile that crept over his white face! He pressed my hand and said, "God bless you! Tell me their names," he asked. He pointed to the stars on the flag.

"The last I know is Ohio. My father lived in Kentucky. But I have guessed Michigan and Indiana and Mississippi— that is where Fort Adams is. That makes twenty.

"But where are your other fourteen? You have not split up any of the old states, I hope?"

Well, that wasn't a bad place to start. I told him the names in the best order I could. He asked me to take down his beautiful map and draw them in with my pencil.

He was wild with delight about Texas. He told me how his brother died there. Then he marked a gold cross where he supposed his brother's grave was. He had guessed about Texas.

Then he was delighted as he saw California and Oregon.

He had suspected those had been added. Though the ships were often there, he had never been permitted to land.

"And the men," said he, laughing, "brought off a good deal besides furs."

Then he went back in time to ask about the *Chesapeake*.[21] He wanted to know what was done to Barron for surrendering her to the *Leopard*.

He also asked if Burr had ever been tried again. He ground his teeth with the only passion he showed.

But in a moment that was over. He said, "God forgive me, for I am sure I forgive him."

Then he asked about the old war. He told me the true story of his fight the day we took the *Java*. And he asked about dear old David Porter.

Then he settled down more quietly and very happily. He waited to hear me tell in an hour the history of fifty years.

How I wished he had somebody there who knew something! But I did as well as I could. I told him of the English war. I told him about Fulton and his steamboat.

I told him about old Scott and Jackson.[22] I told him all I could think about the Mississippi, New Orleans, Texas, and his own old Kentucky.

He asked who was in command of the Legion of the West. I told him it was a very brave officer named Grant. The latest news reported he was about to set up his headquarters in Vicksburg.[23]

[21]The *Chesapeake* was an American ship commanded by James Barron. The ship was attacked in 1807 by the British vessel *Leopard*. Barron surrendered. The English then forced three sailors on the *Chesapeake* to serve on their ship.

[22]Winfield Scott (1786-1866) was a famous army commander and statesman. He assisted Andrew Jackson (1767-1845) during Jackson's presidency (1829-1837).

[23]Ulysses S. Grant (1822-85) was General in Chief of the Union army during the Civil War. Vicksburg was the site of a major battle which Grant won. He later served as president of the U.S. (1869-77).

Then he asked, "Where is Vicksburg?"

I worked that out on the map. It was about a hundred miles above his old Fort Adams. I thought Fort Adams must be a ruin now.

"It must be at old Vick's Plantation," he said. "Well, that is a change!"

I tell you, Ingham, it was a hard thing to **condense** fifty years of history for that sick man. And I do not know now what I told him about foreign newcomers to America.

Nor do I remember what I said about steamboats, railroads, and telegraphs. And I could not recall what I said of inventions, books, colleges, or the military schools.

He interrupted me with the oddest questions you have ever heard. You see, he was just like Robinson Crusoe.[24] Finally he had his chance to ask the **accumulated** questions of fifty-six years!

I remember he asked, all of a sudden, who was president now. When I told him, he asked if Old Abe was the son of General Benjamin Lincoln. He said he had met old General Lincoln at some Indian treaty. Nolan had been just a boy at the time.

I said no. Old Abe was from Kentucky like himself. But I could not tell him of what family. He had worked up from the ranks.

"Good for him!" cried Nolan. "I am glad of that. I thought our danger was in passing on power from one rich family to another."

Then I got to talking about my visit to Washington. I told him of meeting the Oregon Congressman Harding. I told him about the Smithsonian and its exploring expeditions.[25]

---

[24]Robinson Crusoe was a fictional castaway created by Daniel Defoe. Crusoe was shipwrecked on an island for twenty-eight years.
[25]The Smithsonian is a famous scientific and cultural center in Washington, D.C.

I told him about the Capitol and its statues of Liberty and Washington.

Ingham, I told him everything I could think of that would show the greatness and prosperity of his country. But I could not stand to tell him a word about this damned Civil War!

And he drank it in and enjoyed it. I cannot tell you how much he enjoyed it! He grew more and more silent. Yet I never thought he was tired or faint.

I gave him a glass of water. But he just wet his lips and told me not to go away. Then he asked me to bring the *Book of Public Prayer*. He said, with a smile, that it would open at the right place.

It did. There was his double red mark down the page. I knelt down and read, and he repeated it with me.

For ourselves and our country, O gracious God, we thank Thee. We have sinned many times against Thy holy laws. Yet Thou hast never ceased giving us Thy marvelous kindness.

We read to the end of that prayer.

Then he turned to the end of the same book. There I read the words more familiar to me.

We beg Thee to bless Thy servant, the President of the United States, and all others in authority.

And we read the rest of the prayer.

"Danforth," he said, "I have repeated those prayers night and morning. It is now fifty-five years since I began that practice."

Then he said he would go to sleep. He bent me down over him and kissed me. He said, "Look in my Bible, Danforth, when I am gone." And I went away.

But I had not thought it was the end. I thought he was tired and would sleep. I knew he was happy, and I wanted him to be alone.

In an hour, the doctor entered Nolan's cabin gently. He found Nolan had breathed his life away with a smile. He had something pressed close to his lips. It was his father's badge from the Society of Cincinnati.[26]

We looked in his Bible. There was a slip of paper at the place where he had marked the text.

> They desire a country, even a heaven. Therefore, God is not ashamed to be called their God. For He hath prepared for them a city.

On the slip of paper he had written this.

Bury me in the sea. It has been my home, and I love it.

But will someone set up a stone for my memory at Fort Adams or at Orleans? Won't you do this so that my disgrace will not be more than I ought to bear?

Say on it:

In Memory of
PHILIP NOLAN,
Lieutenant in the Army
of the United States.

He loved his country
as no other man loved her.
But no man deserved less
at her hands.

[26]The Society of Cincinnati is made up of men whose ancestors served in the Continental army or navy. The Continental forces were troops who fought for American independence from Britain.

"The Man Without a Country" was first published in 1863.

INSIGHTS INTO
EDWARD EVERETT HALE

(1822-1909)

Hale was once moved to write after hearing a speech by Congressman Clement Vallandigham. The occasion was the Civil War. The Congressman was disgusted with the North. In his speech, he said he did "not want to belong to the U.S."

Hale's answer was "The Man Without a Country." The story created a huge patriotic response. In fact, it was the most discussed story of that troubled period.

Many readers thought "The Man Without a Country" was true. Even some naval officers took it for fact.

Their error is a tribute to Hale's research. He wanted the details of his story to ring true. So he read as many histories as he could find. He even went through all the Navy reports from 1798 to 1861.

But Hale did not want to offend anyone. So he avoided using names of real officers.

Hale slipped up on his main character, however. Too late, he learned a real Philip Nolan had existed. This Nolan had been shot by the Spaniards in 1801. He was viewed as a hero in Texas.

Nolan did not want readers to link his traitor with the real Nolan. His concern led to another work: *Philip Nolan's Friends,* a novel about the Texas hero.

Does the name Hale ring a bell? Edward Everett was the great-nephew of Nathan Hale. Nathan was an American spy hanged by the British during the Revolution. His famous last words were "I only regret that I have but one life to give for my country."

Hale was a Unitarian minister. He preached at the same church in Boston for forty-three years. He also had the honor of serving as chaplain of the U.S. Senate from 1903-1909.

Hale was a man of many causes. He backed the creation of national parks and a world court. He also wanted to introduce profit sharing in business and mass transport systems. He fought for stronger copyright laws, too.

Hale supported many charities, as well. He even founded one. His book *Ten Times One Is Ten* led to the creation of a network of charity clubs.

Other works by Hale:

"My Double, and How He Undid Me," short story

Memories of a Hundred Years, autobiography
and history

A New England Boyhood, autobiography

AN OCCURRENCE AT OWL CREEK BRIDGE

AMBROSE BIERCE

VOCABULARY PREVIEW

Below is a list of words that appear in the story. Read the list and get to know the words before you start the story.

appalling—dreadful; shocking
audible—loud enough to be heard
civilian—person who is not in the military
deflected—turned aside
dignitary—person of high position or rank
dwellings—homes
elude—to escape or avoid
executioner—one who kills a person condemned to death
expelled—released or pushed out
liberal—not strict; open to many views
perspective—the relationship between objects in
   terms of distance, size, position, etc.
random—without a specific plan or aim; hit-or-miss
reluctant—unwilling; not eager
sentinel—guard; lookout
silhouette—a dark shadow or outline seen against a light
   background
sluggish—slow-moving; dragging
suffocation—the act of smothering or choking
temporary—lasting for a limited time
velocity—speed
vigorously—powerfully; forcefully

AN
OCCURRENCE
AT
OWL
CREEK
BRIDGE

The time is the Civil War. Southerner Peyton Farquhar is about to be hanged. But in the space of a second, Peyton manages to slip away from his captors.

Peyton is only allowed to run so far, however. In the end, he again meets up with an old and undefeated enemy.

A man stood upon a railroad bridge in northern Alabama. He looked down into the swift water twenty feet below. The man's hands were behind his back, the wrists tied with a cord. A rope tightly circled his neck. The rope was attached to a sturdy timber above his head. The slack of the rope fell to the level of his knees.

Some loose boards were laid across the railway tracks. They formed a platform for the man and his

AMBROSE BIERCE

executioners. These executioners were two private soldiers of the Federal[1] army. They were directed by a sergeant who in peacetime may have been a deputy sheriff.

A little further away on the **temporary** platform was an armed officer in the uniform of his rank. He was a captain.

A **sentinel** stood at each end of the bridge with his rifle in the position known as "support." That is, the rifle was held upright in front of the left shoulder. The right arm was thrown across the chest. It was a formal and unnatural position that forced men to stand straight.

It did not appear to be the duty of these two men to know what was occurring at the center of the bridge. They merely blocked the two ends of the bridge.

Behind one of the sentinels, nobody was in sight. The railroad ran straight into a forest for a hundred yards. Then it disappeared behind a curve. Doubtless there was an outpost farther along.

The other bank of the stream was open ground. At the top of a small hill was a fort made out of tree trunks. There were narrow holes in the walls for rifles. Through a single wider opening poked the muzzle of a brass cannon. This cannon covered the bridge.

Between the fort and the bridge were the spectators. These onlookers were a single company of infantry[2] men at "parade rest." That is, the butts of their rifles were on the ground, the barrels against the right shoulder, and the hands crossed upon the stock.

A lieutenant stood at the right of the line. The point of his sword touched the ground. His left hand rested on his right.

Except for the group of four at the center of the bridge, not a man moved. The company faced the bridge, staring stonily, motionless. The sentinels, facing the banks of the stream, looked like statues decorating the bridge.

---

[1]The story takes place during the Civil War (1861-65). The Federal army was the army of the North.
[2]Infantry is a group of army soldiers trained to fight on foot.

The captain stood with folded arms, silent. He observed the work of those under his command but did not make a sign. Death is a **dignitary**. When he comes announced he is to be received with respect. In the code of military behavior, silence and rigidness are signs of this respect.

The man who was going to be hanged was about thirty-five years of age. He was a **civilian**—if you could decide that from his clothing, which was that of a planter.

The man's features were good. He had a straight nose, firm mouth, and broad forehead. His long, dark hair was combed straight back. It fell behind his ears to the collar of his well-fitting coat.

The man wore a mustache and pointed beard but no whiskers. His eyes were large and dark gray. They had a kindly expression which was hardly to be expected in one whose neck was in a noose.

Evidently this man was not a common murderer. The **liberal** military code allows for hanging many kinds of people. Gentlemen are not excluded.

The preparations being complete, the two private soldiers stepped aside. Each drew away the plank on which he had been standing. The sergeant turned to the captain, saluted, and placed himself immediately behind that officer. In turn that officer moved apart one pace.

These movements left the condemned man and the sergeant standing on the two ends of the same plank. This plank laid across three of the railroad ties on the bridge. The end on which the civilian stood almost, but not quite, reached a fourth tie.

The plank had been held in place by the weight of the captain. It was now held by that of the sergeant. At a signal from the captain, the sergeant would step aside. Then the plank would tilt and the condemned man would go down between the two ties.

This arrangement seemed simple and effective to the man. His face had not been covered nor his eyes bandaged. He looked a moment at his "unsteady footing." Then he let his gaze wander to the swirling stream racing madly beneath his feet.

A piece of driftwood caught his attention. His eyes followed it down the current. How slowly it appeared to move! What a **sluggish** stream!

The man closed his eyes in order to fix his last thoughts on his wife and children. The water (touched to gold by the early sun), the fort, the soldiers, the driftwood—all had distracted him.

And now he became conscious of a new disturbance. Striking through his thoughts was a sound which he could neither ignore nor understand. It had a sharp, clear, metallic beat like the stroke of a blacksmith's hammer on an anvil. It had the same ringing quality.

He wondered what it was and whether it were distant or near. It seemed both. Its beat was regular but as slow as the ringing of a funeral bell. He awaited each stroke with impatience and—he did not know why—fear.

The periods of silence grew longer and longer. The delays became maddening. The greater the pauses, the more the sounds increased in strength and sharpness. They hurt his ear like the thrust of a knife. He feared he would scream. What he heard was the ticking of his watch.

He unclosed his eyes and saw again the water below him. "If only I could free my hands," he thought. "Then I might throw off the noose and spring into the stream.

"By diving I could dodge the bullets. Then swimming **vigorously**, I could reach the bank, run into the woods, and get home.

"My home, thank God, is still outside their lines. My wife and little ones are still beyond the invaders farthest advances."

As these thoughts flashed into the doomed man's brain, the captain nodded to the sergeant. The sergeant stepped aside.

II

Peyton Farquhar was a well-to-do planter from an old and highly respected Alabama family. He was a slave owner. So like other slave owners, he was a politician.

Naturally he was an original secessionist[3] and deeply devoted to the Southern cause. Urgent circumstances kept him from joining the heroic army that had fought in so many losing battles.

This shameful restraint annoyed him and made him impatient. He longed for action, for the life of a soldier, the chance for glory. He felt that chance would come, as it comes to all in wartime.

Meanwhile, he did what he could. No service was too humble to do to aid the South. No adventure was too risky to undertake. He would do anything that suited a civilian who was at heart a soldier. He believed for the most part that all is fair in love and war.

One evening Farquhar and his wife were sitting on a bench near the entrance of his land. A gray-clad soldier rode up to the gate and asked for a drink of water. Mrs. Farquhar was only too happy to serve him with her own white hands.

While she fetched the water, her husband approached the dusty horseman. Farquhar asked eagerly for news from the front.

"The Yanks are repairing the railroads," said the man. "We are getting ready for another advance. They have reached the Owl Creek bridge and put it in order. They also have built a fort on the north bank.

"The commander has issued an order, which is posted everywhere. He has declared that any civilian caught interfer-

---

[3]A secessionist is one who wants to break away from a larger group. The Confederates were secessionists who wanted the South to break away from the United States.

ing with the railroad, its bridges, tunnels, or trains will be immediately hanged. I saw the order."

"How far is it to the Owl Creek bridge?" Farquhar asked.

"About thirty miles."

"Are there any soldiers on this side of the creek?"

"Only one soldier half a mile out, on the railroad. There is also a single sentinel at this end of the bridge."

"Suppose a man—a civilian and a person familiar with hanging—should make an attempt. Suppose he should **elude** the soldier and perhaps get the better of the sentinel," said Farquhar, smiling. "What could he do?"

The soldier thought a moment. "I was there a month ago," he replied. "I saw that last winter's flood had lodged a pile of driftwood at this end of the bridge. It is now dry and would burn like yarn."

The lady had now brought the water, which the soldier drank. He thanked her politely. Then he bowed to her husband and rode away.

An hour later, after nightfall, he passed the plantation again. He rode northward in the direction from which he had come. He was a Federal scout.

III

As Peyton Farquhar fell straight downward through the bridge, he lost consciousness. He appeared to be like one already dead.

He was awakened from this state—ages later, it seemed—by the pain of a sharp pressure on his throat. This was followed by a sense of **suffocation**. Sharp, painful agonies seemed to shoot from his neck downward through all his body.

These pains flashed along sensitive nerves and hit with an unbelievably rapid beat. The agonies seemed like streams of beating fire, heating him to an unbearable temperature.

As to his head, he was conscious of nothing but a feeling of fullness—of stuffiness. But no thought went along with these sensations. The mental part of his nature was already erased. He had power only to feel, and feeling was torment.

He was conscious of motion. He was now the fiery heart of a glowing cloud. He swung back and forth in huge sweeps like a big pendulum.[4]

Then all at once, with terrible suddenness, the light about him shot upward with a loud splash. A frightful roaring was in his ears. All was cold and dark.

His power of thought was restored. He knew that the rope had broken and he had fallen into the stream. He was not being strangled any further.

But the noose around his neck was already suffocating him. It kept the water from his lungs. To die of hanging at the bottom of a river! The idea seemed ridiculous to him.

He opened his eyes in the darkness. Above him he saw a gleam of light. How distant it seemed, how far out of reach!

He was still sinking as the light became fainter and fainter. Finally it was a mere glimmer. Then it began to grow and brighten. He knew that he was rising toward the surface.

He was **reluctant** to recognize this because now he was very comfortable. "To be hanged and drowned," he thought, "that is not so bad. But I do not wish to be shot. No, I will not be shot. That is not fair."

He was not conscious of an effort. But a sharp pain in his wrist told him he was trying to free his hands. He gave the struggle his attention. But he watched it like one might watch a juggler's tricks—without interest in the outcome.

What splendid effort! What great, superhuman strength! Ah, that was a fine effort! Bravo!

The cord fell away. His arms parted and floated upward. He could see the hands dimly on each side in the growing light.

---

[4]A pendulum is a rod with a heavy end that swings back and forth. The pendulum sets the motion of a clock so it will keep time.

He watched his hands with a new interest as they pounced upon the noose around his neck. They tore it away and thrust it fiercely aside. The twistings of the noose now looked like a water snake.

"Put it back!" He thought he shouted these words to his hands. Undoing the noose had created the greatest pain he had yet experienced.

His neck ached horribly. His brain was on fire. His heart, which had been fluttering faintly, leapt up. It tried to force itself out of his mouth. His whole body was attacked and twisted with unbearable pain!

But his disobedient hands did not listen to the command. They beat the water vigorously with quick, downward strokes. He was forced to the surface.

He felt his head emerge. His eyes were blinded by the sunlight. His chest expanded wildly. With a great and final agony, his lungs swept up a big gulp of air. Instantly, he **expelled** it with a scream!

He now had all his physical senses. Indeed, they were incredibly keen and alert. Something in the awful disturbance of his system had uplifted and refined his senses.

He now experienced things he had never before perceived. He felt the ripples on his face. He heard their separate sounds as they struck. He looked at the forest on the bank, saw each tree, the leaves, and even the veins.

He actually saw the insects on the leaves: the locusts, the colorful flies, and the gray spiders stretching their webs from twig to twig. He noted the rainbow colors in the dewdrops on the million blades of grass.

He heard the gnats dancing above the whirlpools of the stream. He heard the beating of the dragonflies' wings. The strokes of the water spider's legs sounded like oars which moved a boat. All these made **audible** music.

A fish slid along beneath his eyes. He heard the rush of its body parting the water.

He had come to the surface facing down the stream. In a moment, the world seemed to wheel slowly around. He was the center point. He saw the bridge, the fort, the soldiers on the bridge, the captain, the sergeant, the two privates, and his executioners. They were in **silhouette** against the blue sky.

They shouted and gestured, pointing at him. The captain had drawn his pistol but did not fire. The others were unarmed. Their movements were ugly and horrible. Their forms were gigantic.

Suddenly he heard a sharp crack. Something struck the water within a few inches of his head. His face was spattered with spray.

He heard a second crack and saw one of the sentinels with a rifle at his shoulder. A light cloud of blue smoke rose from the muzzle.

The man in the water saw the eye of the man on the bridge gazing into his own through the sights of the rifle. He saw it was a gray eye. He remembered having read that gray eyes were keenest. All famous marksmen had them. Nevertheless, this one had missed.

A whirlpool had caught Farquhar and turned him half around. He was again looking into the forest on the bank opposite the fort.

The sound of a clear, high singsong voice now rang out behind him. It came across the water with a clearness that pierced and overwhelmed all other sounds. It even drowned out the beating of the ripples in his ears.

He was no soldier. But he had been around camps enough to know the fearful meaning of that drawling, steady chant. The lieutenant on shore was taking part in the morning's work.

How cold and unfeeling was their chant. What an even, calm tone—which promised and brought peace to the men. With what regular pauses fell those cruel words:

"Attention, company! . . . Shoulder arms! . . . Ready! . . . Aim! . . . Fire!"

Farquhar dived—dived as deeply as he could. The water roared in his ears like the voice of Niagara.[5] Yet he heard the dulled thunder of the rifle fire.

Rising again toward the surface, he met shining bits of metal sinking. These metal bits, which slowly spun downward, were strangely flattened. Some of them touched him on the face and hands.

Then they fell away, continuing to plunge downward. One stuck between his collar and neck. It was uncomfortably warm and he snatched it out.

As he rose to the surface, gasping for breath, he saw he had been underwater a long time. He could see he was farther downstream—nearer to safety.

The soldiers had almost finished reloading. The metal ramrods flashed as they were drawn from the barrels, turned, and thrust into their sockets. The two sentinels fired again. Each fired separately. Each missed their target.

The hunted man saw all this over his shoulder. He was now swimming vigorously with the current. His brain was as energetic as his arms and legs. He thought as rapidly as lightning.

"The officer," he reasoned, "will not make that thoughtless error a second time. It is as easy to dodge a round of shots as a single shot. He has probably already given the command to fire at will. God help me, I cannot dodge them all!"

An **appalling** splash two yards from him was followed by a loud rushing sound. It seemed to travel back through the air to the fort.

The splash died in an explosion that stirred the river to its depths! A rising sheet of water curved over him. Then it fell down upon him, blinded and strangled him! The cannon had taken a hand in the game.

[5]Niagara is a famous waterfall on the Niagara River. The river lies on the border between the U.S. and Canada.

He shook his head to clear it of the noise. As he did so, he heard the **deflected** shot humming through the air ahead. In an instant it was cracking and smashing the branches in the forest beyond.

"They will not do that again," he thought. "The next time they will use grapeshot.[6]

"I must keep my eye on the gun. The smoke will warn me—the sound of the shot arrives too late. It lags behind the missile. That is a good gun."

Suddenly he felt himself whirled round and round. He was spinning like a top. The water, the banks, the forests, the now-distant bridge, fort, and men were all mixed and blurred. Objects were just colors now. He saw only circular streaks of strips of color.

He had been caught in the center of a huge whirlpool. It was whirling him with a **velocity** that made him dizzy and sick.

In a few moments he was flung upon the gravel at the foot of the left or southern bank. The bank was behind a point which concealed him from his enemies.

Being suddenly at rest and feeling the rough gravel beneath one hand restored him. He wept with delight. He dug his fingers into the sand. Then he threw it over himself in handfuls and audibly blessed it. It looked like diamonds, rubies, emeralds. He could think of nothing beautiful which it did not look like.

The trees on the bank were giant garden plants. The man noted a clear order in their arrangement. He inhaled the perfume of their blooms. A strange, rosy light shone through the spaces among their trunks. The wind in their branches made the music of harps.

He had no wish to perfect his escape. He was content to remain in that enchanting spot until captured.

A whiz and rattle of grapeshot among the branches high above his head woke him from his dream. The cheated man

---

[6]Grapeshot is a bunch of small iron balls that are shot from a cannon.

at the cannon had fired him a **random** farewell. He sprang to his feet and rushed up the sloping bank. There he plunged into the forest.

All that day he traveled. He directed his route by the sun. The forest seemed endless. Nowhere did he discover a break in it—not even a woodman's road.

He had not known that he lived in such a wild region. There was something strange in this discovery.

By nightfall, he was tired, footsore, and starving. The thought of his wife and children urged him on.

At last he found a road which led him in what he knew to be the right direction. It was as wide and straight as a city street.

Yet it seemed untraveled. No fields bordered it. There were no **dwellings** anywhere. Not even the barking of a dog suggested humans lived nearby.

The black bodies of the trees formed a straight wall on both sides. At the horizon the trees came together in a point. The scene was like a diagram to teach **perspective**.

Overhead shone great golden stars. They looked very unfamiliar and seemed to be grouped in strange constellations.[7] He was sure they were arranged in some order which had a secret and evil meaning.

The wood on either side was full of different noises. Once, twice, and again he clearly heard whispers in an unknown language.

His neck was in pain. Lifting his hand to it, he found it horribly swollen. He knew it had a black circle where the rope had bruised it.

His eyes felt puffy. He could no longer close them. His tongue was swollen with thirst. He relieved its fever by thrusting it into the cold air.

But how soft was the grass that carpeted the untraveled avenue. He could no longer feel the roadway under his feet!

No doubt, despite his suffering, he had fallen asleep while

[7]Constellations are stars grouped together in a definite area of the sky.

walking. For now he sees another scene. He stands at the gate of his own home. All is as he left it. All is bright and beautiful in the morning sunshine. He must have traveled the entire night.

He pushes open the gate and walks up the wide white walk. He sees a flutter of female clothes. His wife—looking fresh, cool, and sweet—steps down from the porch to meet him. At the bottom of the steps, she waits. She wears a smile of unspeakable joy and stands with matchless grace and dignity. Ah, how beautiful she is!

He springs forward with extended arms. As he is about to clasp her, he feels a stunning blow on the back of his neck. A blinding white light shines all about him, sounding like a cannon burst. Then all is darkness and silence!

Peyton Farquhar was dead. His body, with a broken neck, swung gently from side to side beneath the Owl Creek bridge.

"An Occurrence at Owl Creek Bridge" was first published in 1890.

INSIGHTS INTO AMBROSE BIERCE

(1842-1914?)

Bierce was 19 when he signed up to fight during the Civil War. His years in the Union Army surely affected him. He was at some of the bloodiest battles in the war.

Later, in his famous *Devil's Dictionary,* Bierce offered these definitions.

Peace: period of cheating between two periods of fighting.

War: by-product of the arts of peace.

Bierce, like many fiction writers of the day, was a journalist for a time. In fact, Bierce had a famous circle of friends among fellow reporters. While working in San Francisco, he knew both Mark Twain and Bret Harte.

He was called "Bitter" Bierce for his sarcasm and black humor. The nickname also matched Bierce's unhappy family life. His marriage ended in divorce. One son was shot to death in a fight over a girl. Another son died of alcoholism.

Bierce's "Prattle" newspaper column was widely quoted around the country. His comments in that column could make or break an author. And Bierce had a way of writing that was not soon forgotten. He once came up with this one-line review: "The covers of this book are too far apart."

continued

Bierce's end is a mystery. In 1913, at the age of 70, he went to Mexico. There he is said to have joined Pancho Villa's side in a Mexican war. He was never heard of again.

Other works by Bierce:

"The Coup de Grace," short story
"The Damned Thing," short story
"A Horseman in the Sky," short story
"The Man and the Snake," short story
The Devil's Dictionary, book

THE PIT AND THE PENDULUM
EDGAR ALLAN POE

VOCABULARY PREVIEW

Below is a list of words that appear in the story. Read the list and get to know the words before you start the story.

abyss—a deep hole that seems bottomless
acute—a narrow angle, less than 90° (opposite of *obtuse,* which is a wide angle, more than 90° but less than 180°)
circuit—the path or distance around a place
descent—a move to a lower level
fatigue—tiredness; weariness
grotesqueness—quality of being odd or bizarre
indistinctly—unclearly or vaguely
ingenuity—cleverness; ability to invent
intensity—degree of power or fierceness
intolerably—unbearably
irregularity—not being regular; unevenness
perceptible—noticeable
perish—to die or be destroyed
ponder—think over; study
ravenous—starving and greedy
relentlessly—in a determined, unyielding way
severed—cut or split
stealthily—in a quiet, secret way
unique—one of a kind; unusual
vapor—gas produced when a solid or liquid is heated

THE PIT AND THE PENDULUM

EDGAR ALLAN POE

In the darkest dungeons of Spain, a man faces tortures out of a nightmare. His tormentors are devilish experts. Their aim is not just to kill their victim. They want to make him long for death.

I was sick—sick to death from long agony. When they finally untied me and I was allowed to sit, I felt that my senses were leaving me. The sentence—the fearful sentence of death—was the last clear sound I heard.

After that, the sound of the inquisitorial[1] voices seemed to blend together in one dreamy,

---

[1]Inquisitorial means questioning. It also refers here to the Inquisition. The Inquisition arrested and tried unbelievers and enemies of the Roman Catholic Church.

vague hum. It brought to my soul the idea of *revolution*.[2] Maybe this was because I imagined it sounded like the whir of a mill wheel.

This only lasted a brief time. Soon I heard no more. Yet, for a while, I saw. But I saw things in an exaggerated way that was horrible!

I remember seeing the lips of the black-robed judges. The lips appeared to me white. They were even whiter than the paper I am writing on.

And they seemed thin, even to the point of **grotesqueness**. They were thin from the **intensity** of being held in an expression of firmness. Thin from being held with fixed determination and with stern contempt for human torture.

I saw that the sentence that was my fate was still coming from those lips. I saw the lips twist with deadly speech. I saw them form the syllables of my name. And I trembled because there was no sound.

For a few moments of feverish horror, I saw the soft and barely noticeable waving of the black drapes. These drapes wrapped the walls of the room.

Then my eyes fell upon the seven tall candles on the table. At first they wore the look of kindness. They seemed like white, slender angels who would save me.

But then, all at once, a deadly sickness came over my spirit. I felt every nerve in my body quiver as if I had touched an electric wire. I watched as the angel forms became ghosts with heads of flame. I saw that there would be no help from them.

Then a thought crept into my mind like a rich, musical note. I thought of what sweet rest there must be in the grave. The thought came gently and **stealthily**. It seemed a long time before I fully understood it.

But just as my spirit grasped the thought, the figures of the judges disappeared, as if by magic. The tall candles sank

[2]Here revolution means the turning of a circle.

into nothingness. Their flames went out completely. The blackness of darkness followed.

All feelings appeared to be swallowed up in a mad, rushing fall. It was like the **descent** of the soul into Hades. Then silence and stillness and night were my universe.

I had fainted. But I still do not think I lost all consciousness. What was left of it, I will not try to define or describe.

Yet all was not lost. In the deepest sleep—no! In feverish insanity—no! In fainting—no! In death—no! Even in the grave, all *is not* lost. Otherwise, there would be no everlasting life for man.

Waking up from the deepest sleep, we break the delicate web of *some* dream. Yet a second later (because the web is so frail), we do not remember we have dreamed.

There are two stages in coming back to life after fainting. The first stage is the awakening of the mind or spirit. The second stage is physical awareness. If we could remember the first stage when we reach the second, we would probably find memories of the gulf beyond.

And that gulf is—what? How at least do we tell its shadows from those of the tomb?

Perhaps we cannot recall the first stage at will. Yet, after a long time, do not the memories come to us on their own? They flow back while we wonder in amazement where they've come from.

The man who has never fainted does not find strange palaces and familiar faces in glowing coals. He does not see things floating in mid-air—the sad visions that most do not see. He does not **ponder** over the perfume of some new flower. He is not bewildered by some music which has never before caught his attention.

Often I have tried to remember. I have struggled to recall some sign of this nothingness my soul had passed into.

There have been moments when I have dreamed of success. There have been brief, very brief periods when I have brought back memories. The clear thinking of a later stage convinces me that they were from that unconscious time.

These shadowy memories tell me **indistinctly** of tall figures that lifted me. In silence, they carried me down—down—still down. Finally a hideous dizziness overcame me at the mere idea of how endless that descent was.

The shadowy memories also tell of a vague horror I felt because of the unnatural stillness of my heart. Then everything suddenly seemed to come to a stop. It was as if this ghastly group who carried me down had gone beyond the limits of the limitless. Finally even they had to pause from their weary labor.

After this, I remember flatness and dampness. And then all is *madness*—the madness of a memory that thinks only about forbidden things.

Very suddenly, motion and sound came back to my soul. I felt the violent motion of my heart. In my ears, I could hear it beating. Then a pause and all is blank. Then sound again and motion and touch—a tingling running through my body. Then the simple awareness, without thought, that I exist. This awareness lasted a long time.

Then, very suddenly, *thought* and terror and an attempt to understand my condition. Then a strong desire to fall back into unconsciousness. A rushing awakening of my soul and a successful effort to move my body.

Now a full memory of the trial, judges, black drapes, sentence, sickness, fainting. Then discovery that I had forgotten all that followed. Time and trying to remember finally allowed me to vaguely recall what happened.

So far, I had not opened my eyes. I felt that I lay on my back, untied. I reached out my hand. It fell heavily on something damp and hard. I left it there for many minutes while I tried to imagine where and *what* I could be.

I wanted to look, but I did not dare. I dreaded the first glance at the objects around me.

It was not that I was afraid to look at horrible things. But I was frightened that there would be *nothing* to see.

Finally, with wild desperation, I quickly unclosed my eyes. My worst fears proved true. The blackness of endless night surrounded me.

I struggled for breath. The intensity of the darkness seemed to weigh me down and strangle me. The air was **intolerably** stuffy.

I still lay quietly and tried to think. I remembered the inquisitorial trial. From that point, I tried to figure out what had happened to me.

The sentence had passed. It seemed to me that a very long time had gone by since then.

Yet I did not think for a moment that I was actually dead. Such a thought, no matter what we read in fiction, cannot be true in real life. But where and in what state was I?

I knew that people who are condemned to death usually **perished** at the *autos-da-fes*.[3] One of these had been held the very evening after my trial. Had I been sent to my cell to wait for the next sacrifice, which would not take place for many months?

I saw at once that this could not be. Victims were wanted immediately. Besides, my dungeon, like those of the condemned at the Toledo prison,[4] had had stone floors. And light had not been shut out altogether.

A fearful thought suddenly drove the blood in a rush to my heart. For a brief period, I once more fell unconscious.

When I recovered after a short time, I got to my feet at once. Every nerve in my body trembled violently. I thrust

[3]*Autos-da-fe* were ceremonies where enemies of the Catholic Church were executed. The condemned were often burned alive.
[4]Toledo is a city in Spain. The prison referred to held those accused by the Inquisition.

my arms wildly above and around me in all directions. I felt nothing.

But still I dreaded to move a step. I feared that I might be stopped by the walls of a *tomb*. Sweat burst from every pore of my body. Drops stood in big cold beads on my forehead.

The agony of suspense finally grew intolerable. I cautiously moved forward with my arms extended. My eyes were straining from their sockets, hoping to see some faint ray of light.

I went on for several steps. Still there was nothing but blackness and emptiness.

I breathed more freely. It seemed clear that my fate was not, at least, the most hideous fate of all.

I still continued to step cautiously forward. As I did so, I now remembered with a rush a thousand vague rumors about the horrors of Toledo. There had been strange things told about the dungeons. I had always considered them to be fables. Yet they were strange and too ghastly to repeat, except in a whisper.

Was I left to perish of starvation in this underground world of darkness? Or was there some fate, perhaps even worse, that awaited me?

I knew that the result would be death—and a death of more than usual bitterness. I knew my judges too well to doubt it. The manner and the time were all that I had left to worry about.

My outstretched hands finally touched something solid. It was a wall that seemed to be made of stone. It was very smooth, slimy, and cold.

I followed this wall. But I stepped with all the care and distrust with which the old stories I had heard filled me.

But this process did not allow me to find out how large my dungeon was. I could make its **circuit** and return to my starting point. Yet I would never realize that since the wall seemed so uniform.

Therefore I hunted for the knife that had been in my pocket when I was taken to the inquisitorial room. But it was gone. My clothes had been replaced with a robe of rough fabric.

I had thought of forcing the knife into some small crack of the stonework. This would have identified my starting point.

The problem was minor. Nevertheless, it seemed impossible to solve at first in my confusion.

Then I tore a part of the hem from my robe. I stretched out the fragment on the floor at an angle to the wall. In feeling my way around the prison, I would not fail to find the rag at the end of the circuit. Or so, at least, I thought.

I had not counted on the large size of the dungeon or on my own weakness. The ground was moist and slippery. I staggered on for some time until I stumbled and fell.

My **fatigue** was so great that I remained there. Sleep soon overtook me where I lay.

When I woke up, I stretched out an arm. I found beside me a loaf of bread and a pitcher of water. I was too exhausted to think about this. I simply ate and drank hungrily.

Shortly afterward, I began my tour around the prison again. With much effort, I at last came back to the piece of fabric. Until I had fallen, I had counted fifty-two paces. When I continued my walk, I counted forty-eight more. Then I found the rag.

There were a hundred paces in all then. Figuring that two paces equaled a yard, I guessed that the dungeon was fifty yards in circuit.

However, I had found many angles in the wall. Thus I could not guess at the shape of the tomb. I could not help thinking of it as a tomb.

I had little purpose—and certainly no hope—in making

these researches. But a vague curiosity influenced me to continue. Leaving the wall, I decided to cross the room.

At first I proceeded with extreme caution. Though the floor seemed solid, it was dangerously slimy.

But finally I became brave and stepped firmly. I tried to cross in as straight a line as possible.

I had advanced ten or twelve steps when the torn hem of my robe got tangled between my legs. I stepped on it and fell violently on my face.

In the confusion of my fall, I failed to notice something startling. But a few seconds later, while I still lay on the floor, it caught my attention.

It was this: my chin rested on the floor of the prison. But the upper part of my head, though hanging lower than my chin, touched nothing. At the same time, my forehead seemed bathed by a clammy **vapor**.

The peculiar smell of rotting fungus[5] arose to my nostrils. I reached forward. I trembled when I found that I had fallen at the very edge of a circular pit. At the moment, of course, I had no way to tell how large it was.

Feeling around the stonework just below the edge, I managed to pull out a small fragment. I let it fall into the **abyss**.

For many seconds I listened to the echoes as it dashed against the sides of the pit. Finally there was a dull plunge into water. Loud echoes followed.

At the same moment, I heard a sound like a door quickly opening and closing overhead. I also saw a faint gleam of light flash suddenly through the gloom. Then it faded away just as suddenly.

I saw clearly the death that had been prepared for me. I congratulated myself for the timely accident that had caused me to escape. One more step and the world would have never seen me again.

---

[5]A fungus is a nongreen plant without leaves, roots, or stems. Mold and mushrooms are examples of fungi.

The kind of death I avoided was like those I heard of in tales about the Inquisition. At the time I had thought they were fables.

I knew there were two possibilities for victims of the Inquisition. The condemned faced death with its most fearful physical agonies. Or they faced the most hideous mental horrors. I had been saved for the second kind.

Long suffering had shattered my nerves. Now I trembled at the sound of my own voice. In every way, I had become a fitting subject for the kind of torture which awaited me.

Shaking all over, I felt my way back to the wall. I decided to perish there rather than risk the terrors of the pits. I now imagined several pits around the dungeon.

In a different state of mind, I might have had the courage to end my misery. By plunging into one of these abysses, I could have ended it all.

But now I was the greatest of cowards. And I could not forget what I had read about these pits. The *sudden* ending of life was not a part of their horrible plan.

My disturbed spirit kept me awake for many long hours. Finally I fell asleep again. When I awakened, I again found a loaf of bread and a pitcher of water by my side. A burning thirst filled me. I emptied the pitcher in one gulp.

It must have been drugged. I had scarcely drunk it before I became extremely drowsy.

A deep sleep fell upon me—a sleep that was like death. I do not know how long it lasted, of course. But when I opened my eyes again, I could see the objects around me. The dungeon was now lit by a wild, yellowish glow. At first I could not see its source.

This light allowed me to see the size and appearance of the prison. I had been greatly mistaken about the size of the room. The whole circuit of its walls was not more than twenty-five yards.

For some minutes, this fact foolishly troubled me. Foolish indeed. What could be less important in this terrible situation than the mere size of my dungeon?

But my mind took a wild interest in trivial matters. So I busily tried to account for the error I made in measurement.

The truth flashed on me at last. In my first exploration, I had counted fifty-two paces up to where I fell. I must then have been within a step or two of the fabric fragment. In fact I had nearly completed the circuit of the tomb. I then slept.

When I awoke, I must have returned the way I had come. This made me think that the circuit was double what it actually was. In my confusion, I had not realized that I began my walk with the wall to the left. And I had ended it with the wall to the right.

I had also been deceived about the shape of the dungeon. In feeling my way, I had found many angles.

Thus I had formed the idea that the shape had great **irregularity**. That is how powerfully total darkness affects someone who is just waking up! The angles were simply a few slight nooks and crannies here and there.

The general shape of the prison was square. What I had taken to be stone now seemed to be iron or some other metal. It covered the walls in huge plates. The seams where the plates were joined together formed the indented spots.

The entire surface of this metal cell was crudely painted. The pictures were hideous, disgusting designs. They were of the kind that monks' superstitions about death produced. Figures of threatening demons, skeletons, and other more fearful images blotted the walls.

I observed that the outlines of these monsters were distinct enough. But the colors seemed faded and blurred, as if from damp air.

I now noticed the floor, too, which was of stone. In the

center yawned the pit from whose jaws I had escaped. But it was the only one in the dungeon.

All of this I saw indistinctly and only with much effort. This was because my position had been greatly changed during my sleep. I now lay stretched out on my back on some kind of low wooden frame.

To this I was tightly tied by a long strap that looked like a saddle belt. It was wrapped many times around my limbs and body. Only my head and left arm, to some extent, remained at liberty. With much effort, I could feed myself from a clay dish that lay beside me on the floor.

I saw, to my horror, that the pitcher had been removed. I say to my horror because I was filled with intolerable thirst. It seemed the plan of my torturers was to increase my thirst. The food in the dish was very spicy meat.

Looking up, I studied the ceiling of my prison. It was some thirty or forty feet up. It was built much like the side walls.

In one of its sections, a very strange figure caught my attention. It was the painted figure of Time as he is usually seen.

But instead of a scythe,[6] he held what seemed to be a huge pendulum.[7] It was the same kind that is seen on old-fashioned clocks.

There was something about this pendulum, however, that made me watch it more carefully. While I gazed directly up at it (because it was right above me), I imagined that I saw it move.

An instant later, I knew it was true. Its swing was brief and, of course, slow.

I watched it for several minutes. I was somewhat fearful but more curious. Wearied at last of watching its dull movement, I looked at the other objects in the cell.

[6]A scythe is a tool with a curved blade used to cut grass or grain. Death is often pictured holding a scythe to "harvest" his victims.

[7]A pendulum is a rod with a heavy end that swings back and forth. The pendulum sets the motion of a clock so it will keep time.

A slight noise attracted my attention. Looking at the floor, I saw several enormous rats crossing it. They had come from the well that lay to my right.

Even while I gazed, they came up in troops. They hurried, with **ravenous** eyes, drawn by the scent of the meat. It required much effort and attention to scare them away from it.

A half an hour or perhaps even an hour passed. (I could not keep track of time very well.) Then I looked up again.

What I saw confused and amazed me. The swing of the pendulum had increased by nearly a yard.

As a result, its speed was also much greater. But what really disturbed me was that it had noticeably *descended*.

I now saw—with horror—that the bottom formed a curved blade of glittering steel. This blade was about a foot from tip to tip. The tips pointed upward, and the lower edge seemed to be as sharp as a razor.

Also like a razor, it seemed huge and heavy. The blade extended upward from the narrow edge into a solid, broad structure. It was attached to a heavy brass rod. The whole thing *hissed* as it swung through the air.

I now knew what death had been prepared for me by the **ingenuity** of those monkish torturers.

The inquisitors knew that I was aware of the pit. *The pit.* Its horrors had been saved for such a bold unbeliever as myself. *The pit.* It was like something out of hell and was said to be the Ultima Thule[8] of their punishments.

I had barely avoided falling into this pit by the merest accident. I knew that surprise, or being trapped, was part of the grotesqueness of death in these dungeons.

Since I had not fallen, it was not part of their devilish plan to hurl me into the abyss. Instead, a different and milder death waited for me.

Milder! I almost smiled at the use of such a word.

---

[8]The ancient island Thule was the point farthest north known to the Romans. Ultima Thule came to mean the farthest point.

What use is it to tell of the long, long hours of cruel horror? During this time, I counted the rushing swings of the steel! Inch by inch—line by line. It descended so slowly that it seemed ages before I saw a difference.

Down and still down it came! Days passed! It might have been many days passed before it swept closely over me. Then, as it fanned me, I felt its bitter breath. The odor of the sharp steel forced itself into my nostrils.

I prayed. I wearied heaven with my plea that the pendulum would descend more quickly. I grew wild and struggled to force myself up against the fearful blade.

And then I suddenly became calm. I lay smiling at the glittering death, like a child looking at some rare jewel.

I had another period of total unconsciousness. It was brief, or seemed so. When I woke again there seemed to have been no **perceptible** descent of the pendulum.

But it might have been a long period. I knew there were evil men who saw me faint. They could have stopped the pendulum's descent.

When I woke up, I felt terribly sick and weak. It was as if I had been starving for a long time. Even through the agonies of that period, I still craved food.

Painfully I stretched out my left arm as far as the bonds permitted. I took the small portion that the rats had spared me. As I took a bite, a half-formed thought of joy and hope rushed to my mind. Yet what business had *I* with hope?

It was, as I said, a half-formed thought. Man has many such thoughts which are never completed. I felt it was of joy and hope. But I also felt it had died even while I was forming it.

In vain I tried to bring it back and complete it. My long suffering had nearly destroyed all my ordinary mental powers. I was a fool—an idiot.

The swings of the pendulum were at right angles to the length of my body. I saw that the blade was positioned to cross the area of my heart. It would tear the fabric of my robe. It would return and repeat this, again and again.

The blade had a very wide sweep of about thirty feet or more. The hissing energy of its descent was enough to break even these walls of iron.

Yet for several minutes, all the blade would do would be to cut my robe. And at this thought, I paused.

I dared not go beyond this thought. I steadily fixed my attention on the idea. It was as if I could stop the descent of the steel by freezing my thoughts.

I forced myself to ponder upon the sound of the blade as it passed across my robe. I thought about the peculiar feeling that the pull of cloth produces on the nerves. I pondered about all of these trivial things until my teeth were on edge.

Down—steadily down it crept. I found mad pleasure in contrasting its speed downward with its speed from side to side.

To the right—to the left. Far and wide—with the shriek of a damned spirit! Toward my heart with the stealthy pace of the tiger! First I laughed and then I screamed as one idea or another ruled me.

Down—certainly, **relentlessly** down! It swung within three inches of my chest!

I struggled violently—furiously—to free my left arm. It was free only from the elbow to the hand. By working hard, I could reach from the plate to my mouth, but no farther.

If I could have broken the straps above the elbow, I would have grabbed and tried to stop the pendulum. I might as well have tried to stop an avalanche!

Down—still without stopping! Still constantly down! I gasped and struggled at each swing. I shrank back wildly at its every sweep. My eyes followed its outward and up-ward swings eagerly with despair. My eyes closed themselves when it swung down.

Yet death would have been a relief. Oh, how unspeakable a relief!

Still I quivered to think how small a sinking of the pendulum would bring that shining axe upon my chest. It was *hope* that made my nerves quiver and my body shrink. It was *hope*—the hope that wins out even in the midst of torture. *Hope* that whispers to those condemned to death even in the dungeons of the Inquisition.

I saw that just ten or twelve swings would bring the steel in contact with my robe. With this observation, my spirit was suddenly filled with the sane calmness of despair. For the first time during many hours—or perhaps days—I *thought*.

It now occurred to me that the bandage or strap that tied me was **unique**. I was not tied by a separate cord. The first stroke of the razor-like blade across any part of the band would cut it. This might allow me to use my left hand to unwind it.

But how fearfully close the blade would be in that case! The result of the slightest struggle could be deadly!

And was it not likely that the torturer's servants had foreseen that this might happen? Wouldn't they have made sure it would not happen? Was it likely that the strap crossed my chest in the path of the pendulum?

Dreading to kill my last hope, I raised my head to get a distinct view of my chest. The strap was tightly wrapped around my body in all directions— *except in the path of the pendulum*.

I had scarcely dropped my head back when a thought flashed in my mind. I can only describe the idea as the unformed half of the rescue plan that I referred to earlier. Only half of the thought had floated through my brain when I raised food to my burning lips.

Now the whole thought was there. It was feeble, scarcely sane, and scarcely fixed. But it was complete. I started to work at once, with the nervous energy of despair.

For many hours, the area around the framework upon which I lay had been swarming with rats. They were wild, bold, and ravenous. Their red eyes glared at me as if they were just waiting for me to lie motionless before they would attack. "What food," I thought, "have they been used to in the pit?"

In spite of my efforts, they had eaten all but a small bit of the food in the dish. I had fallen into continually waving my hand around the plate. But after a while, the movement lost its effect because it was so regular. In their greediness, they often sank their sharp fangs into my fingers.

Now I took the oily, spicy meat that remained. I rubbed the strap wherever I could reach it. Then, raising my hand from the floor, I lay breathlessly still.

At first the ravenous rats were terrified by the change— by the lack of movement. They shrank back in alarm. Many ran toward the pit.

But this was only for a moment. I had not counted on their greediness in vain. Seeing that I was not moving, one or two of the boldest rats jumped up on the framework. They began smelling the strap.

This seemed the signal for the rest to rush forward. Fresh troops hurried from the pit.

They clung to the wood. They poured over it and leaped in hundreds upon me. The regular movement of the pendulum did not disturb them at all. Avoiding its strokes, they worked on the greasy strap.

They pressed and swarmed on me in growing heaps. They squirmed upon my throat. Their cold lips met mine. I was half smothered by the pressure of them.

Disgust that cannot be described swelled within me and chilled my heart. But I felt that in another minute the struggle would be over. I could feel the strap loosening. I knew that it must be **severed** already in more than one place. With a more than human strength of will, I lay *still*.

I had not been wrong about my plan. Nor had my efforts been in vain. Finally, I felt that I was *free*. The strap hung in shreds from my body.

But the stroke of the pendulum already pressed upon my chest. It had split the fabric of the robe. It had cut through the cloth beneath. It swung twice again. A sharp pain shot through every nerve.

But the moment of escape had arrived. With a wave of my hand, my deliverers scuttled away. Then steadily, carefully, and slowly, I slid from the strap and away from the reach of the blade. For the moment, at least, *I was free*!

Free! And in the grasp of the Inquisition! I had scarcely stepped away from my bed of horror when the hellish machine stopped. I saw it being pulled up through the ceiling by some invisible force.

This was a lesson which I took to heart in despair. Without doubt my every move was watched.

Free! I had only escaped one form of agony, to be delivered to another that was worse than death.

With that thought, I nervously looked around at the iron plates that imprisoned me. Something unusual had obviously taken place in the cell.

But this change was not distinct at first. For many minutes of dreamy and trembling thought, I wondered what had happened.

During this period, I discovered where the yellowish light in the cell came from. It came from a crack about half an inch wide. This crack went all around the prison at the base of the walls.

It appeared the walls were completely separated from the floor. I tried—in vain, of course—to look through the crack.

As I got up, the mystery of the change in the cell suddenly dawned on me. I have explained that the outlines of the figures on the walls were distinct enough. Yet the colors had seemed blurred and unclear.

Now these colors were becoming startlingly and intensely brilliant. This gave the ghostly, devilish portraits a look that might have frightened even someone with better nerves. Wild, ghastly demon eyes glared at me from a thousand directions where none had been visible before. They gleamed with the horrid glow of fire. I could not convince myself that this fire was unreal.

Unreal! Even while I breathed, I smelled the vapor of hot iron! A choking odor filled the prison! Every second, the glow in the eyes that glared at my agonies grew deeper! A richer shade of red spread over the pictures of torture.

I panted! I gasped for breath! There was no doubt what my tormentors had planned. Oh, those most unrelenting, most devilish of men!

I shrank from the glowing metal to the center of the cell. I thought of the fiery destruction that was near.

Then the soothing idea of the coolness of the pit came over my soul. I rushed to its deadly brink. I strained my eyes below.

The glare from the burning ceiling lit up the deepest corners. Yet for a wild moment, I refused to understand the meaning of what I saw. Finally, it forced—it wrestled—its way into my soul. It burned itself into my trembling mind.

Oh, for a voice to speak! Oh, horror! Oh, any horror but this!

With a scream, I ran away from the edge. I buried my face in my hands, weeping bitterly.

The heat increased rapidly. Once again, I looked up, shaking as if I had a fever. There had been a second change in the cell. Now the change was obviously in the *form.*

As before, I could not at first understand what was taking place. But I was not left in doubt for long. The Inquisition's revenge had been hurried by my two escapes. There would be no more toying with Death.

The room had been square. I saw that two of its iron angles were now **acute**. As a result, the other two angles had become obtuse. The difference quickly increased with a low rumbling or moaning sound. Instantly the cell had become diamond shaped.

But the change did not stop here. I neither hoped nor desired it to stop. I could have embraced the red walls as a bringer of eternal peace.

"Death," I said, "any death but that of the pit!"

Fool! I should have known that the burning iron was supposed to force me *into the pit*. Could I resist its glow? Or, if even that, could I withstand its pressure?

And now the diamond grew flatter and flatter. This happened so rapidly that I had no time to think about it. Its center and greatest width came just over the yawning pit.

I shrank back. But the closing walls pushed me forward. Finally there was not even an inch left for my burned and twisting body.

I struggled no more. But my agony found release in one long, loud, and final scream. I felt myself tottering on the edge. I looked away—

There was a noisy hum of human voices! There was a loud blast as of many trumpets! There was a harsh, grating sound like that of a thousand thunders!

The fiery walls rushed back! An outstretched arm caught my own as I fell, fainting, into the abyss.

It was General Lasalle.[9] The French army had entered Toledo. The Inquisition was in the hands of its enemies.

---

[9]Antoine Charles Louis Lasalle (1775-1809) was one of Napoleon's generals in the war against Spain. Lasalle led French troops in Spain in 1809. After winning the war, Napoleon ended the Inquisition in Spain.

"The Pit and the Pendulum" was first published in 1843.

INSIGHTS INTO
EDGAR ALLAN POE

(1809-1849)

Poe was both a fine athlete and student in his youth. He once swam six miles in the James River—against the current.

As a student, Poe proved to have a gift for languages. French and Latin were his specialties. But Poe also knew Greek, Spanish, and Italian.

All his life, Poe fought poverty. Once he sent some of his short stories to a publisher. The simple plea "I am poor" was attached.

At one time, Poe was earning only $10 a week (as an editor). He had to support himself, his wife, and mother-in-law on those wages. The family was forced to live on bread and molasses for days.

In 1844, Poe wrote "The Raven." The poem was a great success. It was quickly reprinted everywhere. It was even featured in a high school text.

"The Raven" certainly made Poe famous. But it hardly made him rich. He was paid only five or ten dollars for this timeless favorite.

Poe served as editor and critic on many magazines. Poor wages and a drinking problem often forced Poe to move on.

Yet Poe had a great talent for his work. Sometimes he could be blindly harsh. Often he was brilliant.

The mix served his publishers well. Poe helped increased the readers of one magazine by four times. Another magazine grew by five times during his employment.

continued

Poe married his lovely cousin Virginia Clemm. She was only thirteen—he was twenty-seven—when the wedding took place. Despite the age difference, the Poes were a very loving couple.

Virginia's death in 1847 shook Poe deeply. He cried constantly and stood by her grave for hours.

It was a sad irony that Virginia's death reflected the topic of Poe's own writing. He always said that the greatest subject for a poem was the death of a beautiful woman.

Other works by Poe:

"The Black Cat," short story
"The Gold Bug," short story
"Ligeia," short story
"The Masque of the Red Death," short story
"MS Found in a Bottle," short story
"The Purloined Letter," short story
"The Bells," poem
"To Helen," poem

THE LOTTERY

SHIRLEY JACKSON

VOCABULARY PREVIEW

Below is a list of words that appear in the story. Read the list and get to know the words before you start the story.

assembled—gathered; collected
boisterous—disorderly and noisy
civic—of a city or town
conducted—managed or operated
constructed—built
consulted—sought information or an opinion
defiantly—with a stubborn refusal to accept something
discarded—thrown out
disengaged—freed; detached
duly—in a proper way
formally—in an orderly and solemn manner, often according to custom
interminably—continually; without end
jovial—merry or jolly
paraphernalia—pieces of gear or equipment
perfunctory—routine
petulantly—in a snappish, impatient way
precisely—with a careful, correct manner; with exactness
profusely—lushly and richly
recital—performance featuring singing, dancing, storytelling, etc.
reprimand—scolding

THE LOTTERY

June 27 is a special date for the people of the village. The occasion is the exciting once-a-year event, the lottery.

This lottery is special, too. Everyone can play. Tickets are free. And nobody loses—except the person who wins.

The morning of June 27th was clear and sunny, with the fresh warmth of a full-summer day. The flowers were blossoming **profusely** and the grass was richly green.

The people of the village began to gather in the square, between the post office and the bank, around ten o'clock. In some towns there were so many people that the lottery took two days and had to be started on June 26th.

Shirley Jackson

But in this village there were only about three hundred people. Therefore, the whole lottery took less than two hours. It could begin at ten o'clock in the morning and still be through in time to allow the villagers to get home for noon dinner.

The children **assembled** first, of course. School was recently over for the summer. The feeling of liberty sat uneasily on most of them. They tended to gather together quietly for a while before they broke into **boisterous** play. Their talk was still of the classroom and the teacher, of books and **reprimands**.

Bobby Martin had already stuffed his pockets full of stones. The other boys soon followed his example, selecting the smoothest and roundest stones. Bobby and Harry Jones and Dickie Delacroix—the villagers pronounced his name "Dellacroy"— eventually made a great pile of stones. They built it in one corner of the square and guarded it against the raids of the other boys.

The girls stood aside, talking among themselves, looking over their shoulders at the boys. The very small children rolled in the dust or clung to the hands of their older brothers or sisters.

Soon the men began to gather. They stood surveying their own children, speaking of planting and rain, tractors and taxes. They gathered together, away from the pile of stones in the corner. Their jokes were quiet and they smiled rather than laughed.

The women, wearing faded house dresses and sweaters, came shortly after their menfolk. They greeted one another and exchanged bits of gossip as they went to join their husbands.

Soon the women, standing by their husbands, began to call to their children. The children came reluctantly. Some had to be called four or five times.

Bobby Martin ducked under his mother's grasping hand.

He ran, laughing, back to the pile of stones. His father spoke up sharply, and Bobby came quickly and took his place between his father and his oldest brother.

The lottery was **conducted**—as were the square dances, the teenage club, the Halloween program—by Mr. Summers. He had time and energy to devote to **civic** activities. He was a round-faced, **jovial** man and he ran the coal business. People were sorry for him because he had no children and his wife was a scold.[1]

When Mr. Summers arrived in the square, carrying the black wooden box, a murmur rose among the villagers. He waved and called, "Little late today, folks."

He was followed by the postmaster, Mr. Graves, who carried a three-legged stool. The stool was put in the center of the square and Mr. Summers set the black box down on it.

The villagers kept their distance, leaving a space between themselves and the stool. When Mr. Summers said, "Some of you fellows want to give me a hand?" there was a hesitation. Then two men—Mr. Martin and his oldest son, Baxter—came forward. They held the box steady on the stool while Mr. Summers stirred up the papers inside it.

The original **paraphernalia** for the lottery had been lost long ago. The black box on the stool had been put into use even before Old Man Warner, the oldest man in town, was born.

Mr. Summers spoke frequently to the villagers about making a new box. But no one liked to upset even as much tradition as was represented by the black box. There was a story that the present box had been made with some pieces of the previous box. That box had been **constructed** when the first people settled down to make a village here.

Every year after the lottery, Mr. Summers began talking again about a new box. But every year the subject was allowed to fade off without anything being done.

The black box grew shabbier each year. By now it was

---

[1]Scold is a noun here and means a woman who scolds or a shrew.

no longer completely black. It had splintered badly along one side to show the original wood color. In some places it was faded or stained.

Mr. Martin and his son held the black box securely on the stool until Mr. Summers had stirred the papers thoroughly with his hand. Because so much of the ritual had been forgotten or **discarded**, Mr. Summers had successfully switched to slips of paper. These slips were substituted for the chips of wood that had been used for generations.

Chips of wood, Mr. Summers had argued, had been all very well when the village was tiny. But now the population was more than three hundred and likely to keep on growing. It was necessary to use something that would fit more easily into the black box.

The night before the lottery, Mr. Summers and Mr. Graves made up the slips of paper and put them in the box. The box was then taken to the safe of Mr. Summers' coal company. There it was locked up until Mr. Summers was ready to take it to the square next morning.

The rest of the year, the box was put away. Sometimes it was stored in one place, sometimes another. It had spent one year in Mr. Grave's barn. Another year it had been underfoot in the post office. Sometimes it was set on a shelf in the Martin grocery and left there.

There was a great deal of fussing to be done before Mr. Summers declared the lottery open. There were the lists to make up. Heads of families, heads of households, and members of each household had to be written down.

Then there was the proper swearing-in of Mr. Summers by the postmaster, as the official of the lottery. Some people remembered that at one time there had been a **recital** of some sort. It had been performed by the official of the lottery. The recital had just been a **perfunctory**, tuneless chant that had been rattled off **duly** each year.

Some people believed that the official used to stand just so when he said or sang the chant. Others believed that he was supposed to walk among the people. But years and years ago this part of the ritual had been allowed to lapse.

There had been, also, a ritual salute. The official of the lottery had had to use it to address each person who came up to draw from the box. This also had changed with time. Now it was felt necessary only for the official to speak to each person approaching.

Mr. Summers was very good at all this. He stood there in his clean white shirt and blue jeans, with one hand resting carelessly on the black box. He seemed very proper and important as he talked **interminably** to Mr. Graves and the Martins.

Just as Mr. Summers finally left off talking and turned to the assembled villagers, Mrs. Hutchinson arrived. She came hurriedly along the path to the square, her sweater thrown over her shoulders. She slid into place in the back of the crowd.

"Clean forgot what day it was," she said to Mrs. Delacroix, who stood next to her. They both laughed softly.

"Thought my old man was out back stacking wood," Mrs. Hutchinson went on. "Then I looked out the window and the kids was gone. Then I remembered it was the twenty-seventh and came a-running."

She dried her hands on her apron, and Mrs. Delacroix said, "You're in time, though. They're still talking away up there."

Mrs. Hutchinson craned her neck to see through the crowd. She found her husband and children standing near the front. She tapped Mrs. Delacroix on the arm as a farewell and began to make her way through the crowd.

The people separated good-humoredly to let her through. Two or three people said, in voices just loud enough to be heard across the crowd, "Here comes your Missus, Hutchinson" and "Bill, she made it after all."

Mrs. Hutchinson reached her husband. Mr. Summers, who had been waiting, said cheerfully, "Thought we were going to have to get on without you, Tessie."

Mrs. Hutchinson said with a grin, "Wouldn't have me leave m'dishes in the sink, now, would you, Joe?" Soft laughter ran through the crowd as the people stirred back into position after her arrival.

"Well, now," Mr. Summers said soberly, "guess we better get started. Get this over with, so's we can go back to work. Anybody ain't here?"

"Dunbar," several people said. "Dunbar, Dunbar."

Mr. Summers **consulted** his list. "Clyde Dunbar," he said. "That's right. He's broke his leg, hasn't he? Who's drawing for him?"

"Me, I guess," a woman said. Mr. Summers turned to look at her.

"Wife draws for her husband," Mr. Summers said. "Don't you have a grown boy to do it for you, Janey?"

Mr. Summers and everyone else in the village knew the answer perfectly well. Yet, it was the business of the official of the lottery to ask such questions **formally**.

Mr. Summers waited with an expression of polite interest while Mrs. Dunbar answered.

"Horace's not but sixteen yet," Mrs. Dunbar said regretfully. "Guess I gotta fill in for the old man this year."

"Right," Mr. Summers said. He made a note on the list he was holding. Then he asked, "Watson boy drawing this year?"

A tall boy in the crowd raised his hand. "Here," he said. "I'm drawing for m'mother and me." He blinked his eyes nervously and ducked his head as several voices in the crowd said "Good fellow, Jack" and "Glad to see your mother's got a man to do it."

"Well," Mr. Summers said, "guess that's everyone. Old Man Warner make it?"

"Here," a voice said, and Mr. Summers nodded.

A sudden hush fell on the crowd as Mr. Summers cleared his throat and looked at the list.

"All ready?" he called. "Now, I'll read the names—heads of families first. The men come up and take a paper out of the box. Keep the paper folded in your hand without looking at it until everyone has had a turn. Everything clear?"

The people had done it so many times that they only half listened to the directions. Most of them were quiet, wetting their lips, not looking around. Then Mr. Summers raised one hand high and said, "Adams."

A man **disengaged** himself from the crowd and came forward.

"Hi, Steve," Mr. Summers said, and Mr. Adams said, "Hi, Joe." They grinned at one another humorlessly and nervously. Then Mr. Adams reached into the black box and took out a folded paper. He held it firmly by one corner as he turned and went hastily back to his place in the crowd. There he stood a little apart from his family, not looking down at his hand.

"Allen," Mr. Summers said. "Anderson. . . .Bentham."

"Seems like there's no time at all between lotteries any more," Mrs. Delacroix said to Mrs. Graves in the back row. "Seems like we got through with the last one only last week."

"Time sure goes fast," Mrs. Graves said.

"Clark. . . .Delacroix."

"There goes my old man," Mrs. Delacroix said. She held her breath while her husband went forward.

"Dunbar," Mr. Summers said. Mrs. Dunbar went steadily to the box while one of the women said, "Go on, Janey." Another said, "There she goes."

"We're next," Mrs. Graves said. She watched while Mr.

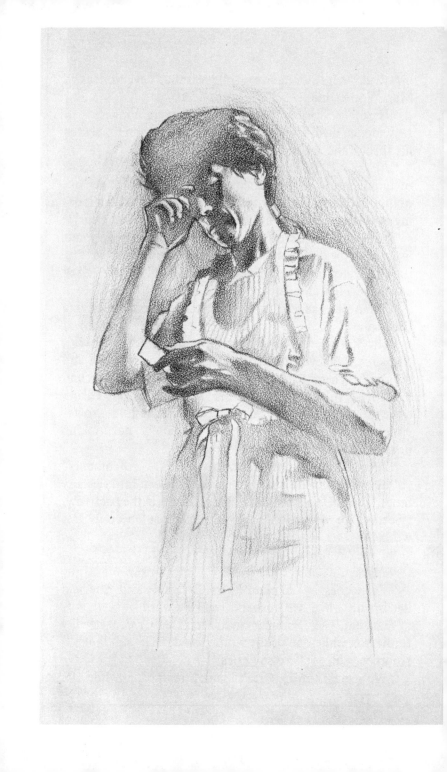

Graves came around from the side of the box. He greeted Mr. Summers gravely and selected a slip of paper from the box.

By now all through the crowd there were men holding the small folded papers in their large hands. Many were turning them over and over nervously. Mrs. Dunbar and her two sons stood together, Mrs. Dunbar holding the slip of paper.

"Harburt. . . .Hutchinson."

"Get up there, Bill," Mrs. Hutchinson said. The people near her laughed.

"Jones."

"They do say," Mr. Adams said to Old Man Warner, who stood next to him, "that over in the north village they're talking of giving up the lottery."

Old Man Warner snorted. "Pack of crazy fools," he said. "Listening to the young folks, nothing's good enough for *them*. Next thing you know, they'll be wanting to go back to living in caves, nobody work any more, live *that* way for a while.

"Used to be a saying about 'Lottery in June, corn be heavy soon.' First thing you know, we'd all be eating stewed chickweed[2] and acorns.

"There's *always* been a lottery," he added **petulantly**. "Bad enough to see young Joe Summers up there joking with everybody."

"Some places have already quit lotteries," Mrs. Adams said.

"Nothing but trouble in *that*," Old Man Warner said boldly. "Pack of young fools."

"Martin." And Bobby Martin watched his father go forward.

"Overdyke. . . .Percy."

"I wish they'd hurry," Mrs. Dunbar said to her older son. "I wish they'd hurry."

[2]Chickweed is a common weed often eaten by birds.

"They're almost through," her son said.

"You get ready to run tell Dad," Mrs. Dunbar said.

Mr. Summers called his own name. He stepped forward **precisely** and selected a slip from the box. Then he called, "Warner."

"Seventy-seventh year I been in the lottery," Old Man Warner said as he went through the crowd. "Seventy-seventh time."

"Watson." The tall boy came awkwardly through the crowd. Someone said, "Don't be nervous, Jack," and Mr. Summers said, "Take your time, son."

"Zanini."

After that, there was a long pause, a breathless pause. Finally Mr. Summers held his slip of paper in the air and said, "All right, fellows."

For a minute no one moved. Then all the slips of paper were opened. Suddenly all the women began to speak at once, saying, "Who is it?" "Who's got it?" "Is it the Dunbars?" "Is it the Watsons?"

Then the voices began to say, "It's Hutchinson. It's Bill." "Bill Hutchinson's got it."

"Go tell your father," Mrs. Dunbar said to her older son.

People began to look around to see the Hutchinsons. Bill Hutchinson was standing quiet, staring down at the paper in his hand.

Suddenly Tessie Hutchinson shouted to Mr. Summers, "You didn't give him time enough to take any paper he wanted. I saw you. It wasn't fair."

"Be a good sport, Tessie," Mrs. Delacroix called. Mrs. Graves said, "All of us took the same chance."

"Shut up, Tessie," Bill Hutchinson said.

"Well, everyone," Mr. Summers said, "that was done pretty fast. Now we've got to be hurrying a little more to get done in time."

He consulted his next list. "Bill," he said, "you draw for the Hutchinson family. You got any other households in the Hutchinsons?"

"There's Don and Eva," Mrs. Hutchinson yelled. "Make *them* take their chance!"

"Daughters draw with their husbands' families, Tessie," Mr. Summers said gently. "You know that as well as anyone else."

"It wasn't *fair,*" Tessie said.

"I guess not, Joe," Bill Hutchinson said regretfully. "My daughter draws with her husband's family, that's only fair. And I've got no other family except the kids."

"Then, as far as drawing for families is concerned, it's you," Mr. Summers said in explanation. "And as far as drawing for households is concerned, that's you, too. Right?"

"Right," Bill Hutchinson said.

"How many kids, Bill?" Mr. Summers asked formally.

"Three," Bill Hutchinson said. "There's Bill, Jr., Nancy, and little Dave. And Tessie and me."

"All right, then," Mr. Summers said. "Harry, you got their tickets back?"

Mr. Graves nodded and held up the slips of paper. "Put them in the box, then," Mr. Summers directed. "Take Bill's and put it in."

"I think we ought to start over," Mrs. Hutchinson said, as quietly as she could. "I tell you it wasn't *fair*. You didn't give him time enough to choose. *Every*body saw that."

Mr. Graves had selected the five slips and put them in the box. He dropped all the papers but those onto the ground. The breeze caught the discarded papers and lifted them off.

"Listen, everybody," Mrs. Hutchinson was saying to the people around her.

"Ready, Bill?" Mr. Summers asked. Bill Hutchinson,

with one quick glance around at his wife and children, nodded.

"Remember," Mr. Summers said, "take the slips and keep them folded until each person has taken one. Harry, you help little Dave."

Mr. Graves took the hand of the little boy who came willingly with him up to the box. "Take a paper out of the box, Davy," Mr. Summers said. Davy put his hand into the box and laughed.

"Take just *one* paper," Mr. Summers said. "Harry, you hold it for him."

Mr. Graves took the child's hand and removed the folded paper from the tight fist. He held it while little Dave stood next to him and looked up at him wonderingly.

"Nancy next," Mr. Summers said. Nancy was twelve, and her school friends breathed heavily as she went forward, switching her skirt. She took a slip daintily from the box.

"Bill, Jr.," Mr. Summers said. Billy, his face red and his feet over-large, nearly knocked the box over as he got a paper out.

"Tessie," Mr. Summers said. She hesitated for a minute, looking around **defiantly**. Then she set her lips and went up to the box. She snatched a paper out and held it behind her.

"Bill," Mr. Summers said. Bill Hutchinson reached into the box and felt around. He brought his hand out at last with the slip of paper in it.

The crowd was quiet. A girl whispered, "I hope it's not Nancy." The sound of the whisper reached the edges of the crowd.

"It's not the way it used to be," Old Man Warner said clearly. "People ain't the way they used to be."

"All right," Mr. Summers said. "Open the papers. Harry, you open little Dave's."

Mr. Graves opened the slip of paper. There was a general

sigh through the crowd as he held it up and everyone could see that it was blank.

Nancy and Bill, Jr., opened theirs at the same time. Both beamed and laughed. They turned around to the crowd and held their slips of paper above their heads.

"Tessie," Mr. Summers said. There was a pause. Then Mr. Summers looked at Bill Hutchinson, and Bill unfolded his paper and showed it. It was blank.

"It's Tessie," Mr. Summers said, and his voice was hushed. "Show us her paper, Bill."

Bill Hutchinson went over to his wife and forced the slip of paper out of her hand. It had a black spot on it. It was the black spot Mr. Summers had made the night before with the heavy pencil in the coal-company office. Bill Hutchinson held it up, and there was a stir in the crowd.

"All right, folks," Mr. Summers said. "Let's finish quickly."

The villagers had forgotten the ritual and lost the original black box. But they still remembered to use stones. The pile of stones the boys had made earlier was ready. There were stones on the ground with the blowing scraps of paper that had come out of the box.

Mrs. Delacroix selected a stone so large she had to pick it up with both hands. She turned to Mrs. Dunbar. "Come on," she said. "Hurry up."

Mrs. Dunbar had small stones in both hands. She said, gasping for breath, "I can't run at all. You'll have to go ahead and I'll catch up with you."

The children had stones already. Someone gave little Davy Hutchinson a few pebbles.

Tessie Hutchinson was in the center of a cleared space by now. She held her hands out in despair as the villagers moved in on her. "It isn't fair," she said. A stone hit her on the side of the head.

Old Man Warner was saying, "Come on, come on,

everyone." Steve Adams was in the front of the crowd of villagers. Mrs. Graves was beside him.

"It isn't fair, it isn't right," Mrs. Hutchinson screamed. Then they were upon her.

"The Lottery" was first published in 1948.

INSIGHTS INTO
SHIRLEY JACKSON

(1919-1965)

Jackson's story "The Lottery" was an overnight sensation. Jackson received letters—many of them angry—about it for the rest of her life.

The tale was even banned in South Africa. But Jackson accepted the action with pride. She remarked that at least the South Africans understood the story.

Much of Jackson's work was about the supernatural. She used to joke that she was the only practicing witch in New England.

But there was a serious side to Jackson's beliefs. Once she was angered by her publisher, Alfred Knopf. During this time, she learned that Knopf would soon be skiing in Vermont, near her home. So Jackson made a wax image of a man. Then she stuck a pin in its leg.

Knopf's trip ended in a broken leg. Jackson felt sure she caused the injury.

Jackson and her husband, Stanley Edgar Hyman, were book collectors. Jackson gathered 500 books on witchcraft alone. Some were even written in languages she could not read.

She was also a mystery story fan. She would raid the local bookstores and bring back dozens of editions. All told, the Hymans' collection totaled more than 30,000 volumes.

Four children, five cats, two dogs, plus birds, fish, and a hamster. Those were the members of the Jackson household at one time.

continued

As a devoted housewife, Jackson took care of them all. Friends were amazed to find her with a batch of cookies baked by eight in the morning.

Even through those busy years of the 1950s, Jackson wrote steadily. During that time, she published forty-four tales, six articles, two autobiographies, one children's book, and four novels.

Other works by Jackson:

"Charles," short story

"The Daemon Lover," short story

"One Ordinary Day with Peanuts," short story

The Haunting of Hill House, novel

Life Among the Savages, autobiography

We Have Always Lived in the Castle, novel

THE GIFT OF THE MAGI

O. HENRY

VOCABULARY PREVIEW

Below is a list of words that appear in the story. Read the list and get to know the words before you start the story.

agile—quick and spry (nimble)
ardent—having heartfelt emotions; passionate
assertion—declaration or claim
chronicle—history; account
coax—lure or persuade
conception—idea; notion
coveted—desired
craved—longed or hungered for
discreet—cautious or tactful in behavior
duplication—copy or double
ecstatic—delighted; overjoyed
garment—piece of clothing
implied—suggested; expressed in an indirect way
mammoth—huge; gigantic
nimble—lively and quick (agile)
prudence—caution and shrewdness
ransacking—searching thoroughly; rummaging
subsiding—dying off or slackening
truant—absent without permission
unassuming—humble and meek

THE GIFT OF THE MAGI

O. HENRY

Della and Jim are a poor, young couple. They live in a shabby apartment on $20 a week. What do they possibly have to give each other for Christmas? Even in the early 1900s, $1.87 doesn't go far.
The gifts Della and Jim finally choose for each other turn out to be both worthless and beyond price.

One dollar and eighty-seven cents. That was all. And sixty cents of it was in pennies. Pennies saved one and two at a time by bullying the grocer, vegetable man, and butcher. Bargaining until your cheeks burned. Knowing that you were silently being accused of cheapness, as such petty dealing **implied**.

Three times Della counted it. One dollar and eighty-seven cents. And the next day would be Christmas.

There was clearly nothing to do but flop down on the shabby little couch and howl. So Della did it. Which brings up the moral that life is made up of sobs, sniffles, and smiles. Mostly sniffles.

While the lady of the house is gradually **subsiding** from the first stage to the second,[1] take a look at the home. A furnished flat[2] at $8 per week.

It would not exactly have gone begging for a description. Yet the police might have hauled it in for sticking out the hat for a kind word or two.[3]

In the hall below was a letterbox into which no letter would go. There was an electric button, too. No human finger could **coax** a ring from it. A card underneath bore the name "Mr. James Dillingham Young."

The "Dillingham" had been flung out onto the breeze during an old period of wealth. At the time, its owner was being paid $30 per week.

Now the income had shrunk to $20. And the letters of "Dillingham" looked blurred. They seemed as though they were thinking seriously of shrinking to a modest, **unassuming** D.

But whenever Mr. James Dillingham Young came home to his flat, he was called "Jim." Moreover, he was warmly hugged by Mrs. James Dillingham Young. She's already been introduced to you as Della. Which is all very good.

Della finished her cry and fixed her cheeks with the powder puff. Standing by the window, she looked out dully. She stared at a grey cat walking a grey fence in a grey backyard.

Tomorrow would be Christmas Day. She had only $1.87 with which to buy Jim a present. She had been saving every penny she could for months. And this was the result.

[1] Della is going from sobs to sniffles.
[2] Flat is another word for apartment.
[3] The author is hinting that the apartment is shabby.

Twenty dollars a week doesn't go far. Expenses had been greater than she had figured. They always are.

Only $1.87 to buy a present for Jim. Her Jim. Many a happy hour she had spent planning for something nice for him. Something fine and rare and silver. Something just a little bit near to being worthy of the honor of being owned by Jim.

There was a mirror between the windows of the room. Perhaps you have seen a mirror in an $8 flat. A very thin and **agile** person might get a fairly accurate **conception** of his looks. That is if he observed his reflection in a rapid series of strips. Being slender, Della had mastered the art.

Suddenly she whirled from the window and stood before the glass. Her eyes were shining brilliantly. But her face had lost its color within twenty seconds. Rapidly she pulled down her hair and let it fall to its full length.

Now there were two possessions of the James Dillingham Youngs in which they both took a mighty pride. One was Jim's gold watch that had been his father's and his grandfather's.

The other was Della's hair. Had the Queen of Sheba[4] lived in the flat across the way, Della would have let her hair hang out the window to dry. That would have shown just how little Her Majesty's jewels and gifts were worth.

And had King Solomon been the janitor, with all his treasures piled in the basement, Jim would have pulled out his watch each time he passed. Then the old King would have plucked at his beard in envy.

So now Della's beautiful hair fell about her. Rippling and shining, it tumbled like a waterfall of brown waters. It reached below her knee, becoming almost a **garment** for her. And then Della put it up again nervously and quickly.

Once she hesitated for a minute. A tear or two splashed on the worn red carpet while she stood still there.

---

[4]The Queen of Sheba and King Solomon are wealthy, wise monarchs in the Bible.

On went her old brown jacket. On went her old brown hat. With a whirl of skirts and the brilliant sparkle still in her eyes, she fluttered out the door. Then she went down the stairs to the street.

She finally stopped at a sign. "Madame Sofronie. Hair Products of All Kinds," it read.

One flight up Della ran. There she collected herself, panting. Madame—large, too white, and chilly—hardly looked like a "Sofronie."

"Will you buy my hair?" asked Della.

"I buy hair," said Madame. "Take yer hat off. Let's have a sight at the looks of it."

Down rippled the brown waterfall.

"Twenty dollars," said Madame. She lifted the mass with a practiced hand.

"Give it to me quick," said Della.

Oh, and the next two hours tripped by on rosy wings. Forget the mixed metaphor. Della was **ransacking** the stores for Jim's present.

She found it at last. It surely had been made for Jim and no one else. There was no other like it in any of the stores. She knew because she had searched high and low in all of them.

It was a platinum watch chain, simple and clean in design. As all good things do, it properly announced its value by substance alone. It did not depend on gaudy decoration. It was even worthy of The Watch.

As soon as she saw it, she knew that it must be Jim's. It was like him. Quietness and value. The description applied to both.

Twenty-one dollars they took from her for it. She hurried home with the eighty-seven cents. With that chain, Jim might be properly anxious about the time in any company. Grand as the watch was, he sometimes had to sneak a look at it. The old leather strap he used in place of a chain embarrassed him.

When Della reached home, her delight gave way a little to **prudence** and reason. She got out her curling irons. Then she lighted the gas and went to work repairing the damages made by generosity and love. That is always a tremendous task, dear friends—a **mammoth** task.

Within forty minutes her head was covered with tiny, tight curls. She looked remarkably like a **truant** schoolboy.

Della gazed at her reflection in the mirror. She looked at it long, carefully, and critically.

"If Jim doesn't kill me before he takes a second look at me," she said to herself, "he'll say I look like a Coney Island chorus girl.[5]

"But what could I do? Oh, what could I do with $1.87?"

At seven o'clock the coffee was made. The frying pan was on the back of the stove, hot and ready to cook the chops.

Jim was never late. Della doubled the watch chain in her hand. Sitting on the corner of the table near the door that he always entered, she waited.

Then she heard his step on the stair away down on the first flight. She turned white for just a moment.

Della had a habit of saying little silent prayers about the simplest everyday things. Now she whispered, "Please God, make him think I am still pretty."

The door opened. Jim stepped in and closed it. He looked thin and very serious.

Poor fellow, he was only twenty-two. And to be burdened with a family! He needed a new overcoat and he was without gloves.

Jim stopped inside the door. He halted in his tracks, like a setter scenting quail. His eyes were fixed upon Della. There was an expression in them that she could not read.

[5]Coney Island is a beachfront area of New York City. Cheap amusement halls are one attraction of the island.

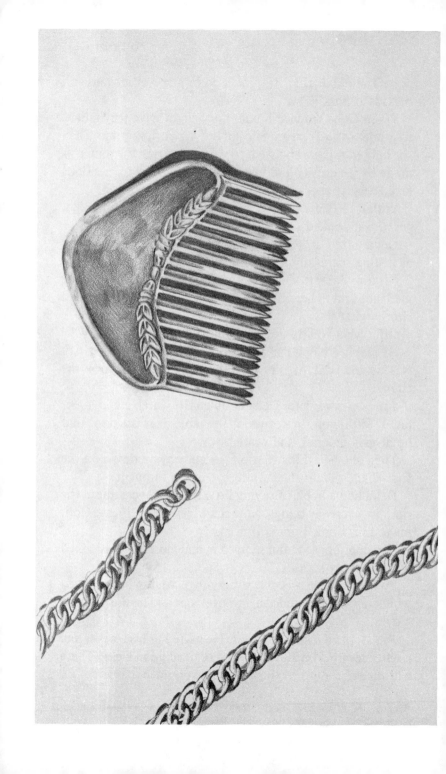

That expression terrified her. It was not anger, surprise, disapproval, or horror. Nor was it any of the emotions that she had been prepared for. He simply stared at her with that peculiar expression on his face.

Della wriggled off the table and ran to him.

"Jim, darling," she cried, "don't look at me that way. I had my hair cut off and sold it. I couldn't have lived through Christmas without giving you a present.

"It'll grow out again. You won't mind, will you? I just had to do it. My hair grows awfully fast.

"Say 'Merry Christmas!' Jim, and let's be happy. You don't know what a nice—what a beautiful, nice gift—I've got for you."

"You've cut off your hair?" asked Jim with an effort. It seemed as if he had not grasped that obvious fact even after the hardest mental labor.

"Cut if off and sold it," said Della. "Don't you like me just as well, anyhow? I'm me without my hair, ain't I?"

Jim looked about the room curiously.

"You say your hair is gone?" he said with an air almost of an idiot.

"You needn't look for it," said Della. "It's sold, I tell you—sold and gone, too. It's Christmas Eve, boy. Be good to me. I sold it for you.

"Maybe the hairs of my head were numbered," she went on with a sudden serious sweetness. "Yet nobody could ever count my love for you. Shall I put the chops on, Jim?"

Jim seemed quickly to wake out of his trance. He wrapped his arms around his Della. For ten seconds let us regard with **discreet** attention some trivial object in the other direction.

Eight dollars a week or a million a year—what is the difference? A mathematician or a comic would give you the wrong answer. The magi brought valuable gifts, but that was not among them.[6] More light will fall on this dark **assertion** later on.

---

[6]The magi are three wisemen in the Bible who brought gifts to Jesus Christ in honor of his birth.

Jim took a package from his overcoat pocket and threw it upon the table.

"Don't make any mistake about me, Dell," he said. "I don't think there's any haircut, shave, or shampoo that could make me like my girl any less. But if you'll unwrap that package, you may see why you had me going a while."

White, **nimble** fingers tore at the string and paper. And then an **ecstatic** scream of joy. Then, alas! a quick female change to wild tears and wails. All the comforting powers of the lord of the flat were immediately called for.

For there lay The Combs. It was the set that Della had worshipped for so long in a window on Broadway. Beautiful combs, pure tortoise shell, with jeweled rims. Just the shade to wear in the beautiful but now vanished hair.

They were expensive combs, she knew. Her heart had simply **craved** and longed for them without the least hope of getting them. And now they were hers. But the hair that should have adorned the **coveted** combs was gone.

Still, she hugged them to her bosom. At last she was able to look up. With dim eyes and a smile she said, "My hair grows so fast, Jim!"

And then Della leaped up like a little burned cat. She cried, "Oh, oh!"

Jim had not yet seen his beautiful present. She held it out to him eagerly upon her open palm. The dull precious metal seemed to flash with a reflection of her bright, **ardent** spirit.

"Isn't it a dandy, Jim? I hunted all over town to find it. You'll have to look at your watch a hundred times a day now. Give me your watch. I want to see how it looks on it."

Instead of obeying, Jim tumbled down on the couch. There he put his hands under the back of his head and smiled.

"Dell," said he, "let's put our Christmas presents away and keep 'em awhile. They're too nice to use right now. I sold the watch to get the money to buy your combs. And now suppose you put the chops on.''

The magi, as you know, were wise men—wonderfully wise men—who brought gifts to the Babe in the manger. They invented the art of giving Christmas presents. Being wise, their gifts were no doubt wise ones. Possibly the gifts could even have been exchanged in case of **duplication**.

And here I have lamely told you the uneventful **chronicle** of two foolish children in a flat. Both most unwisely sacrificed for each other the greatest treasures of their house.

But a last word to the wise of these days. Let it be said that of all who give gifts, these two were the wisest. Of all who give and receive gifts, people like these are wisest. Everywhere they are wisest. They are the magi.

''The Gift of the Magi'' was first published in 1905.

INSIGHTS INTO
O. HENRY

(1862-1910)

O. Henry was a skillful artist. Even as a boy, he would amuse himself by sketching his teacher with one hand. With the other hand, he would be solving a math problem.

His talent was so promising that several friends wanted to pay his way to art school. O. Henry always refused. To him, drawing was an amusing hobby, not his lifework.

Among O. Henry's other talents were singing; playing the guitar, mandolin, and piano; sharp shooting; and cooking. One of his favorite recipes was for onions soaked in vinegar. He eagerly urged all his dinner guests to try it.

O. Henry's writing career began while he was serving time in an Ohio prison for taking money from a bank. Partly to buy things for his daughter, Margaret, O. Henry sent out stories to magazines.

O. Henry was just a pen name. The author's real name was William Sydney Porter.

So where did the pen name come from?

The author claimed he took it from a register used by druggists. This story could be true because there was an O. Henry listed in the register.

Another story was told by a girlfriend of O. Henry. She said a cat was the source of the name. "Henry the Proud" would not appear if simply summoned with "Henry!" He would only come when called by "Oh (or O.) Henry."

O. Henry once agreed to write a Christmas story for the *New York Sunday World*. Since a color drawing was planned, the tale had to be finished quickly for the artist to review. But O. Henry dragged his feet.

At last the artist went to O. Henry and asked for the tale. O. Henry admitted he hadn't even thought up the plot. He finally pulled an image out of thin air for the artist.

More deadlines passed. Still no story. On the last possible day, a *World* reporter appeared. He again begged for the story. But O. Henry hadn't begun it yet.

O. Henry told the reporter to lie down on the couch. He said that the reporter would become the model for the hero of the tale.

After three hours of steady writing, "The Gift of the Magi" was completed.

Some critics complain that O. Henry's characters are too romantic and not realistic. But in one case, the reality of O. Henry's life seems more dramatic than his fiction.

When O. Henry fled the country to avoid jail in 1896, his wife loyally supported him. Athlo was gravely sick during this time. Yet she made a lace handkerchief and sold it for twenty-five dollars.

With the money, Athlo prepared a box of Christmas gifts for her husband. O. Henry later learned that she packed the box while suffering a fever of 105°.

It was Athlo's ill health that brought O. Henry back to the U.S—and to prison. She died five months after his return.

Her image lives on in fiction. Della in "The Gift of the Magi" is said to be based on Athlo.

Other works by O. Henry:
    "Friends in San Rosario," short story
    "The Last Leaf," short story
    "The Ransom of Red Chief," short story
    "A Retrieved Reformation," short story

THE LEGEND OF SLEEPY HOLLOW

WASHINGTON IRVING

VOCABULARY PREVIEW

Below is a list of words that appear in the story. Read the list and get to know the words before you start the story.

abundance—an amount that is more than enough; plenty
adjacent—nearby; neighboring
amorous—showing sexual interest or love (*amours* mean love affairs)
ample—plentiful
authentic—real or true
chivalrous—like an ideal knight: brave, noble, and courteous
conscientious—honest and honorable
diligent—done with great care and effort
dismal—gloomy and dreary
esteemed—appreciated; valued
extract—something separated from something else
famine—great lack of food in an area
formidable—frightening and awesome
frolic—prank or merry entertainment
gallant—heroic and courteous
lateral—of or to the side
petty—minor; unimportant
rustic—country or rural (usually with overtones of being simple and even backward)
specter—ghost
vicinity—neighborhood; nearby region

THE LEGEND OF SLEEPY HOLLOW

Washington Irving

> *Good food, pretty women, and eerie ghost stories. That's the sum of schoolmaster Ichabod Crane's desires. So what happens when Ichabod samples his three greatest pleasures? And all on one night? He gets the scare of his life!*

In one of those roomy coves on the east shore of the Hudson River there lies a small market town or port. This town is at a widening of the river. The ancient Dutch explorers called it the Tappan Zee. There they always wisely shortened sail and begged the protection of St. Nicholas[1] when they crossed.

The small town or port is called by some Greensburgh. But it is more generally and properly known by the name of Tarrytown.

This name was given in the old days by the good housewives of the **adjacent** country. They called it Tarrytown because their husbands liked to linger about the village tavern on market days.

---

[1] St. Nicholas is a Christian saint who is said to guard sailors.

Be that as it may, I don not swear it is true. I merely refer to it to be precise and **authentic**.

Not far from Tarrytown, about two miles away, there is a little valley among high hills. It is one of the quietest places in the whole world. A small brook glides through the valley with just enough murmur to lull you to sleep. The occasional whistle of a quail or the tapping of a woodpecker is almost the only sound that ever breaks the peace.

As a boy, I recall doing my first squirrel hunting there. I hunted in a grove of tall walnut trees that shades one side of the valley. I had wandered into it at noon when all of nature is strangely quiet.

I was startled by the roar of my own gun as it broke the stillness around. The noise was repeated by the angry echoes.

If ever I should wish for a quiet place to hide from the noisy world, I would choose this little valley. I do not know of a better place to quietly dream away the rest of a troubled life.

This out-of-the-way glen has long been known by the name of SLEEPY HOLLOW. And its **rustic** lads are called the Sleepy Hollow Boys by everyone around. The place gets its name from its quietness. It also owes its name to the strange character of the people, whose ancestors were the original Dutch settlers.

A drowsy, dreamy mood seems to hang over the land. It even seems to seep into the very atmosphere.

Some say the place was bewitched by a German doctor in the early days of the settlement. Others say that an old Indian chief, the wizard of his tribe, held his powwows there. This is said to have occurred even before Master Hendrick Hudson discovered the country.

In any case, it is certain that the place is still controlled by some witching power. Magic holds a spell over the minds of good people. It causes them to walk in a continual daydream.

The people also hold all sorts of strange beliefs. And they are subject to trances and visions. Often they see strange sights and hear music and voices in the air.

The whole neighborhood is filled with local tales, haunted spots, and twilight superstitions. Stars shoot and meteors glare more often across the valley than anywhere else. And it is a favorite place for the romps of the nightmare,[2] with her nine children.

But the chief spirit that haunts this enchanted region and seems to command the others is a headless ghost on horseback. Some say it is the ghost of a Hessian trooper.[3]

It is believed that the trooper's head was carried away by a cannonball during the revolutionary war. He is often seen by the county folk as he hurries along in the gloom of night. He flies as if he were on the wings of the wind.

This headless ghost doesn't not always stay in the valley. Sometimes he extends his rides to the nearby roads. He especially rides in the **vicinity** of a church not far away.

Some authentic historians have carefully collected and sorted the floating factors about this **specter**. They claim the trooper was buried in the churchyard. They say he rides forth each night to the scene of the battle in search of his head. The rushing speed of his ride strikes like a midnight blast. He is in a hurry to get back to the church before dawn.

That, at any rate, is the general substance of this superstition. It has furnished material for many a wild story in that region of shadows. And by all the country firesides, the specter is known by the name of the Headless Horseman of Sleepy Hollow.

It is remarkable that not just natives of the valley have this tendency to see visions. Anyone who lives there for a time also soon develops it.

These newcomers may have been wide awake before they

[2]Nightmare here means a demon who travels with nine spirits, said to be her children. She torments sleepers.

[3]The British hired German troops to fight Americans during the Revolution. These soldiers were called Hessians.

entered that sleepy region. But in a little time, they are sure to breathe in the bewitching air. Then they begin to grow imaginative, dream dreams, and see ghosts.

I mention this peaceful spot with all possible praise. It is in such small, forgotten Dutch valleys of New York that population, manners, and customs stay fixed. The great wave of moving and progress continually makes changes in the rest of the restless country.

But change sweeps by unnoticed in these valleys. They are like the little pools of still water which border a rapid stream. There you can see a straw or bubble quietly bobbing or slowly spinning while the stream rushes on.

Many years have passed since I walked through the drowsy shades of Sleepy Hollow. Yet I think I still might find the same trees and families growing in that sheltering place.

In a remote period of American history—that is, some thirty years ago—there was a worthy man named Ichabod Crane. He lived (or as he put it, "tarried"[4]) in Sleepy Hollow. He was there to instruct the children of the neighborhood.

Ichabod was a native of Connecticut. That state supplies the Union with pioneers for the mind as well as the forest. Every year it sends forth many frontier woodsmen and country schoolmasters.

Crane's name suited him. He was tall but extremely thin. He had narrow shoulders and long arms and legs. His hands dangled a mile out of his sleeves. His feet could have served for shovels. His whole frame was loosely hung together.

Ichabod's head was small and flat on top. He had huge ears and large, green, glassy eyes. His long, pointed nose looked like a weathervane perched on his skinny neck to show which way the wind blew.

Ichabod was quite a sight striding along on a windy day with his clothes fluttering. You might have mistaken him

[4]Ichabod is playing on the meaning of tarry ("to linger") and the name Tarrytown.

for the spirit of **famine**. Or you might have thought he was some scarecrow who had eloped from a cornfield.

Ichabod's schoolhouse was a low building with one large room. It was crudely built out of logs. The windows were partly glass, partly pages of old copybooks.

The school was very cleverly locked when not in use. A strong twig was twisted in the doorhandle. Stakes set against the shutters secured the windows. This way, a thief might enter easily, but he would have a hard time getting out. Yost Van Houten, the builder, probably borrowed the stake idea from the design of the eel trap.

The schoolhouse stood in a lonely but pleasant spot at the foot of a woody hill. A brook ran close by. At one end of the building grew a birch tree.

From here you might hear the low murmur of pupils' voices reciting their lesson on a drowsy summer day. They were interrupted now and then by the commanding voice of the schoolmaster. His voice could be heard, issuing a threat or an order.

Sometimes an even more horrifying noise could be heard. This was the sound of a birch switch. Ichabod used it to urge a tardy pupil along the flowery path of knowledge.

Truth to tell, Ichabod was a **conscientious** man. He always kept in mind the golden rule, "Spare the rod and spoil the child." Ichabod Crane's pupils certainly were not spoiled.

But I don't want you to imagine that Ichabod was one of those cruel rulers of the school. He didn't enjoy causing his subjects pain.

On the contrary, Ichabod was fair rather than harsh. He took the burden off the backs of the weak and laid it on those of the strong.

Those weakling boys who ducked whenever the switch was even raised were forgiven. But not so with little, tough, wrongheaded Dutch boys who grew even tougher after a beating. They were given double blows.

Ichabod called all this "doing his duty" to the children's parents. And he never punished without offering great comfort to the aching child. He always assured the child that "he would remember it and thank him for it as long as he lived."

After school, Crane was even the companion and playmate of the larger boys. On holiday afternoons he would walk some of the smaller ones home. He chose those who had pretty sisters or mothers who were good cooks.

Indeed, it was wise of Ichabod to keep on good terms with his pupils. He did not make much money as a teacher. It would have been scarcely enough to supply him with daily bread. Ichabod was a huge feeder. Though he was thin, he could swallow huge meals like a snake.

It was the custom in those parts to give the schoolmaster food and lodging. So to help meet expenses, Ichabod stayed with the farmers whose children he taught. He lived a week at one farm, then a week at the next. Thus he made the rounds of the neighborhood with all his belongings tied up in a handkerchief.

This might have been a burden on the pockets of his rustic supporters. They are likely anyway to view schooling as too costly and teachers as mindless workers.

But Ichabod had ways of making himself both useful and agreeable. He helped the farmers with the lighter farmwork. He made hay and mended fences. He also took horses to water, drove the cow to pasture, and cut firewood.

Ichabod put aside, too, the dignity and authority he used to rule his little school. He became wonderfully gentle and pleasant.

Mothers liked him because he praised their children, especially the youngest. The bold lion was pictured lying beside the lamb in the reading book. Likewise Ichabod sat with a child on one knee and rocked a cradle with his foot for long hours.

In addition to his other jobs, Ichabod was also singing master of the neighborhood. He picked up many bright shillings[5] by teaching children hymns.

Ichabod was proud to take his place in front of the choir on Sundays with a band of chosen singers. There, in his own mind, he outshone the preacher.

Certainly his voice was louder than all the others in the church. There are still some strange tones that can be heard a half mile off, on the other side of the millpond. These notes are said to be truly descended from the nose of Ichabod Crane.

Thus by various little clever ways—commonly known as "by hook and by crook"—the worthy teacher got on well enough. In fact, some thought he had a wonderfully easy life of it. But those who thought so did not understand the labor of a schoolmaster's work.

The schoolmaster is generally an important man with the women in any rural neighborhood. He is considered an idle gentleman. His taste and talents are considered greatly superior to those of rough country lovers. Indeed, he is thought to be inferior in learning only to the parson.

His appearance is apt to create a stir at the tea table. The ladies are likely to bring an extra dish of cakes or candies. They may even parade the silver teapot.

Therefore, our schoolmaster was especially fortunate in receiving the smiles of all the country ladies. How he would stand out among them in the churchyard between services on Sundays! He would meet them on Sundays and walk with them along the adjacent millpond.

Ichabod would gather grapes for the ladies from wild vines that overran the trees. Or he might recite verses on the tombstones to amuse them. Sometimes he strolled with a whole flock of them along the banks of the millpond.

Meanwhile, the more bashful country bumpkins hung

[5]A shilling is a British coin.

back sheepishly. They could only envy Ichabod's superior elegance and way of speaking.

From his wandering life, the schoolmaster had also become a kind of traveling newspaper. He carried the whole load of local gossip from house to house. Naturally he was always warmly greeted.

Moreover, the women **esteemed** Ichabod as a man of great learning. He had read several books all the way through. And he knew by heart Cotton Mather's *History of New England Witchcraft*. He believed in that book, by the way, most firmly and strongly.

In fact, Ichabod was oddly both shrewd and foolishly trustworthy. His appetite for the fantastic and his ability to absorb it were equally amazing. And both had been increased by living in this spellbound region. No tale was too far-fetched for him to swallow.

After school, it was often Ichabod's delight to stretch out beside the little brook that whimpered by his school. There he would read over old Mather's fearful tales. He would stay there until the darkness of evening gathered. Finally he would leave when the printed page was a mere mist before his eyes.

Then Ichabod would make his way through swamp, stream, and fearful wood to the farm where he stayed. As he walked, every sound of nature at that witching hour fluttered his excited imagination.

He would jump at the moan of the whippoorwill from the hillside. The sinister cry of the tree toad—the warning signal of a storm—alarmed him. The dreary hooting of the screech owl had the same effect. The sudden rustling of birds, frightened from their roost, would make him jump.

The fireflies, too, now and then startled Ichabod when an uncommonly bright one streamed across his path. And if a huge beetle blundered into him, poor fool was ready to give up the ghost. He was sure he had been struck by a witch.

Ichabod's only way to drown out thought or drive away evil spirits was to sing hymns. People were often filled with awe at hearing his nasal tones floating from a distant hill or dusky road.

Another of Ichabod's pleasures was to pass long winter evenings with the old Dutch wives. They would sit spinning by the fire, with a row of apples roasting. And Ichabod would listen to their marvelous tales.

The wives would speak of ghosts and goblins. They told of haunted fields and brooks and bridges and houses. They particularly talked about he headless horseman or Galloping Hessian of the Hollow as he was sometimes called.

In turn, Ichabod would delight them with his stories of witchcraft. He would tell them of frightful signs and sights and sounds in the air in Connecticut. He would frighten them dreadfully with theories about comets and shooting stars. And he told them the alarming fact that the world did absolutely turn around. Half the time they were topsy-turvy!

All this might have been pleasant. It was fun to snuggle and cuddle in the chimney corner that glowed from a wood fire. Of course no specter dared to show his face there.

But Ichabod paid dearly for this pleasure by the terrors of his walk home afterwards. What fearful shapes and shadows waited by his path in the dim, ghostly glare of a snowy night!

With what longing did he eye everything trembling ray of light from distant windows! How often was he terrified by some shrub covered with snow! He was certain if was a sheeted specter!

How often did he shrink at the sound of his own steps on the frosty crust! How he dreaded to look over his shoulder! He knew there must be some horrid being trampling close behind him!

And how often was he terrified by some rushing blast, howling along the trees! He was certain that it was the Galloping Hessian on his nightly search.

But all these things were mere terrors of the night—phantoms of the mind that walk in darkness. Ichabod had seen many specters in his time. And he had been tempted by Satan in many shapes. But daylight put an end to all these evils.

Ichabod might have passed a pleasant life, in spite of the devil and all his works. But he met up with a being that puzzles man more than ghosts, goblins, and all the witches put together. He crossed the path of a woman.

Among Ichabod's musical pupils who met once each week to learn hymns was Katrina Van Tassel. Katrina was the daughter and only child of a well-to-do Dutch farmer.

Katrina was a fresh, blooming girl of eighteen, as plump as a partridge. She was as ripe, melting, and rosy-cheeked as one of her father's peaches. She was known throughout the region not only for her beauty but her fortune.

Katrina was a little bit of a flirt. You could see this even in her dress. Her clothes were a mix of ancient and modern fashions which best suited her charms.

Katrina wore ornaments of pure yellow gold. Her great-great-grandmother had brought the jewels over from Amsterdam.

Katrina also wore the tempting stomacher[6] of olden times. And she favored short petticoats. She liked to display the prettiest foot and ankle in the region.

Ichabod Crane had a soft and foolish heart when it came to women. It is no surprise that so tempting a tidbit soon found favor in his eyes. This was especially true after he visited Katrina in her father's mansion.

Old Baltus Van Tassel was a perfect picture of a thriv-

[6]A stomacher is a decorative covering once worn by women. It covered the breasts and stomach.

ing, contented, generous farmer. It is true he seldom thought about anything outside his own farm. But there everything was snug, happy, and in good condition.

Van Tassel was satisfied with his wealth but not proud of it. He prided himself on the hearty **abundance** of his farm, not the style in which he lived.

Van Tassel's stronghold was on the banks of the Hudson. He built it in one of those green, sheltered, rich nooks that Dutch farmers like to nest in. A great elm tree spread its broad branches over it.

At the foot of the trees bubbled up a spring of the softest and sweetest water. It flowed into a little well formed of a barrel. Then it stole sparkling away through the grass to meet a neighboring brook. There the joined brooks bubbled along among alders and dwarf willows.

Close to the farmhouse was a huge barn that might have served for a church. The flail[7] busily echoed within the barn from morning till night.

Swallows and martins skimmed twittering about the eaves of this big barn. And rows of pigeons enjoyed the sunshine on the roof. Some sat with their heads under their wings or buried in their feathers. Others swelled, cooed, and bowed to their ladies.

Sleek, slippery porkers were grunting in the peaceful abundance of their pens. Now and then, troops of baby pigs marched about as if to sniff the air.

A stately squadron[8] of snowy geese was swimming in a nearby pond. Whole convoys of ducks also swam there.

Regiments of turkeys were gobbling through the farmyard. Guinea hens fretted about with snappish cries. The flock acted like ill-tempered housewives.

The **gallant** rooster strutted before the barn door. He was the model of a husband, warrior, and fine gentleman. He clapped his reddish-brown wings and crowed with pride and happiness.

---

[7]A flail is a tool used to separate the seeds of grain from the stalk.
[8]Squadron, convoy, and regiment are all military units.

Sometimes this rooster tore up the earth with his feet. Then he generously called to his ever-hungry wives and children. He offered the tidbits he had discovered for them to enjoy.

The teacher's mouth watered as he looked upon this rich promise of tasty winter meals. He pictured to himself every roasting pig running about with a pudding in his belly and an apple in his mouth. The pigeons were snugly put to bed in a comfortable pie. A cover of crust tucked them in.

The geese were swimming in their own gravy. The ducks were paired cozily in dishes like snug married couples. He pictured them with a good helping of onion sauce.

He imagined the future pieces of bacon and juicy, tasty ham when he saw the porkers. Not a turkey went by that Ichabod didn't see it daintily tied up. He pictured its gizzard under its wing with perhaps sausages for a necklace.

Ichabod even saw the bright rooster sprawling on his back in a dish with uplifted claws. The **chivalrous** bird may have refused pity while alive. But it seemed as though he were begging for mercy now that he was dead.

As the dreaming Ichabod imagined this, he took in the rest of the scene. He rolled his great green eyes over the fat meadows around Van Tassel's warm house.

He looked at the rich fields of wheat, rye, buckwheat, and Indian corn. He surveyed the orchard loaded with red fruit.

Ichabod's heart longed for the girl who was to inherit this land. His imagination expanded with the idea that the land might easily be turned into cash. He dreamed how the money could be invested in huge areas of wild land and palaces in the wilderness.

Indeed, in his busy imagination, Ichabod's hopes were already fulfilled. He saw the blooming Katrina with a whole family of children. They were mounted on top of a wagon loaded with household goods. Pots and kettles dangled beneath.

And Ichabod saw himself. He was riding a pacing mare with a colt at her heels. He and his family were setting out for Kentucky, Tennessee, or the Lord knows where.

When Ichabod entered the house, his heart was completely won. It was one of those roomy farmhouses with a high, sloping roof. It was built in the style handed down from the first Dutch settlers.

The low overhanging eaves formed a porch in front. This could be closed up in bad weather. Under the eaves hung flails, harness, various farming tools, and fishing nets.

Benches were built along the sides of the porch for summer use. A great spinning wheel stood at one end. A butter churn stood at the other. These two tools showed the various uses of this important porch.

From this porch the wondering Ichabod entered the hall. The hall formed the center of the mansion. Here the family was usually to be found.

In this hall, dazzling rows of splendid pewter[9] were arranged on a long dresser. A huge bag of wool stood in one corner, ready to be spun. In another stood some linen and wool fresh from the loom.

Ears of Indian corn and strings of dried apples and peaches hung in garlands on the walls. They were mingled with bright red peppers.

A door left ajar gave Ichabod a peep into the best parlor. There he saw claw-footed chairs and dark wooden tables that shone like mirrors. Fireplace pokers, plus a shovel and tongs, gleamed from their hiding place among the plants.

Mock oranges and seashells decorated the mantelpiece. Strings of different colored birds' eggs were draped above it. A great ostrich egg was hung from the center of the room.

A cupboard in the corner had been left open on purpose.

[9]Pewter is a metal made of a mix of tin with lead, copper, or other metals.

It displayed an immense treasure of old silver and well-mended china.

From the moment Ichabod laid his eyes upon these delights, his peace of mind was gone. His only concern was how to gain the affections of the Van Tassels' unequaled daughter.

However, he had more difficulties with this task than knights of olden times had. A knight seldom had anything to battle but giants, witches, fiery dragons, and other such easily defeated foes. He merely had to make his way through the castle gates of iron and brass. Then, passing through the walls of diamond, he would reach the room where the lady was locked.

The knight was able to do all this as easily as a man could carve into a Christmas pie. Then the lady gave him her hand as a matter of course.

Ichabod, on the contrary, had to win his way to the heart of a country flirt. Her heart was a maze of whims and impulses. This continually presented Ichabod with new difficulties and blocks.

And Ichabod had to face an army of fearful foes of real flesh and blood. These were Katrina's many rustic admirers. They kept a watchful and angry eye upon each other. But they were ready to fly out together against any new suitor.

Among the suitors, the most **formidable** was a big, roaring, merrymaking buck. He was called Abraham Van Bunt. His first name, according to Dutch custom, was shortened to Brom.

Brom was the hero of the neighborhood. His deeds of strength and toughness were spoken of everywhere.

Brom had broad shoulders and double joints. His hair was short, curly, and black. He had a rough but not unpleasant face. You could see a mixed air of fun and pride in his features.

Because of his big build and great strength, he had earned

the nickname BROM BONES. He was generally known by that name.

Brom was famous for his great knowledge and skill in horsemanship. He was as nimble on horseback as a Tartar.[10] He was first at all races and cockfights.

Because physical strength is so highly valued in rustic life, he was the umpire in all arguments. He would set his hat on one side and give his decisions. He spoke his mind with an air and tone that forbid any objections or appeals.

Brom was always ready for either a fight or a **frolic**. But he was more full of mischief than ill will. For all his roughness, he had a strong dash of witty good humor at heart.

Brom had three or four close friends who regarded him as their model. At the head of this group, Brom would attend every feud or party for miles around.

In cold weather, you could tell Brom by his fur cap. A bobbing foxtail topped this hat. When folks at a gathering spotted the hat among a squad of riders, they stood ready for a storm.

Sometimes Brom's crew would be heard dashing along past farms at midnight. Whooping and yelling, they sounded like a troop of Cossacks.[11]

The noise would startle the old ladies out of their sleep. They would listen for a moment until the hubbub had clattered by. Then they would exclaim, "Ay, there goes Brom Bones and his gang!"

The neighbors looked upon Brom with a mix of awe, admiration, and goodwill. When any madcap prank or rustic fight occurred in the vicinity, they would shake their heads. They were certain that Brom Bones was at the bottom of it.

The madcap hero had for some time singled out Katrina as the object of his crude affection. In his **amorous** gestures,

[10]Tartars were Asian warriors who attacked parts of Asia and eastern Europe in the 1200s and 1300s. They were famous horseman and fierce soldiers.
[11]A Cossack was a peasant soldier of Russia.

Brom was about as gentle as a bear. Yet it was whispered that Katrina did not altogether discourage his hopes.

At any rate, Brom's appearance was the signal for rivals to retreat. They felt no desire to cross a lion in his amours. When Brom's horse was seen tied to Van Tassel's fence, it was taken as a sure sign that his master was courting or "sparking." Then all other suitors passed by in despair and fought the war on other fronts.

This was the formidable rival with whom Ichabod Crane had to contend. All things considered, a braver man than Ichabod would have shrunk from the contest. A wiser man would have despaired.

But Ichabod was lucky in that he was both flexible and stubborn. He was in form and spirit like a cane of reed. He was yielding but tough. Though he bent, he never broke. He bowed beneath the slightest pressure. But what happened when that pressure was removed? Why, then Ichabod immediately stood tall and carried his head as high as ever.

For Ichabod to have openly competed against his rival would have been madness. Brom was not a man to cross in his amours.

Therefore, Ichabod made his advances in a quiet, gentle, sly manner. He made frequent visits to the farmhouse under cover of his job as singing teacher.

So often the meddling of parents is a stumbling block to lovers. But Ichabod had nothing to fear. Balt Van Tassel was an easy, kind soul. He loved his daughter better even than his pipe. So, like a reasonable man and an excellent father, he let her have her way in everything.

Mrs. Van Tassel, too, had enough to do with her housekeeping and managing her birds. As she wisely said, ducks and geese are foolish things. They must be looked after. But girls can take care of themselves, she said.

Thus the busy woman would bustle about the house or work her spinning wheel at one end of the porch. Meanwhile, honest Balt would sit smoking his pipe at the other end. He would watch the victories of a little wooden warrior who bravely fought the wind with a sword atop the barn.

In the meantime, Ichabod would court the daughter by the side of the spring under the elm. Or they would stroll along in the twilight. That hour is known to be the most favorable to lover's speech.

I do not pretend to know how women's hearts are wooed and won. To me they have always been something to be puzzled over and admired.

Some seem to have but one tender point or doorway. Others seem to have a thousand avenues. They can be captured in a thousand ways.

It is a great victory of skill to gain the heart of a cold woman. But it is still a greater proof of skill to keep the tenderhearted woman. Then a man must battle for his stronghold at every door and window. He who wins a thousand common hearts deserves some fame. But he who keeps the complete affection of a flirt is a hero indeed.

It is certain that the formidable Brom Bones did not have Katrina's complete devotion. From the moment Ichabod made his advances, Brom's standing was lowered. His horse was no longer seen at the fence on courting nights. A deadly feud gradually rose between him and the teacher of Sleepy Hollow.

Brom had a degree of rough chivalry in his nature. He would have liked to have led matters to open warfare. He wanted to settle their claims to the lady. And he wanted to do it in single combat like those clear, simple reasoners, the knights of old.

But Ichabod was too conscious of his foe's superior might to answer the challenge. He had overheard Bones boast that he would "double the schoolmaster up and put him on a shelf in the school." He was too wary to give Brom Bones that chance.

There was something very provoking in Ichabod's stubborn peacefulness. It left Brom no choice but to use his fund of rustic humor. He was forced to play practical jokes on his rival. Ichabod became the butt of many pranks played by Bones and his gang of rough riders.

They began to disrupt Ichabod's once peaceful life. They smoked out his singing school by blocking up the chimney.

They also broke into the school at night, in spite of its formidable locks. Then they turned everything topsy-turvy. The poor schoolmaster began to think that all the witches in the country held their meetings there.

But what was still more annoying, Brom began ridiculing Ichabod in front of Katrina. Brom had a scoundrel dog whom he taught to whine in the most ridiculous manner. The dog served as Ichabod's rival in teaching Katrina hymns.

Matters went on this way for some time. Yet Brom's tricks had no real effect on the situation between the two rivals.

One fine fall afternoon, Ichabod sat thoughtfully on a lofty stool. From this throne he usually watched all the business of his little literary kingdom.

In his hand, Ichabod swayed a ruler. This staff symbolized his complete power over the schoolroom. The birch switch of justice rested on three nails behind the throne. It was a constant terror to evildoers.

On the desk before him could be seen different forbidden items and weapons taken from idle boys. There were half-munched apples, popguns, tops, fly cages, and paper roosters.

Apparently some horrifying sentence of justice had just been given out. Now most of the students were busily intent upon their books. A few slyly whispered, keeping one eye on the teacher. A kind of buzzing stillness filled the room.

The quiet was suddenly interrupted by the appearance of a Negro in a yarn jacket and trousers. He wore a fragment of a hat like the cap of Mercury.[12] He was mounted on the back of a ragged, wild, half-broken colt which he guided with a rope.

The black man came clattering up to the school door. There he delivered Ichabod an invitation to attend a merry-making or "quilting party." The party was to be held that evening at Mr. Van Tassel's.

The man delivered his message. Like all servants on **petty** errands, he spoke with an air of importance and an effort at fine language. Then he dashed over the brook. He was seen scampering away up the Hollow, full of the importance of his errand.[13]

All was bustle and hubbub in the once quiet room. The students were hurried through their lessons without stopping at little things.

Those who were quick skipped over half of the lesson without punishment. But it was a different story with those who were tardy. They had a smart rap in the rear now and then to speed them up or help them over a big word.

Books were tossed aside without being put away on the shelves. Inkstands were overturned. Benches were thrown down. The whole school was turned loose an hour before the usual time. The students burst forth like an army of young imps. They yelped and charged about the meadow in joy at their early release.

The gallant Ichabod now spent at least an extra half hour in dressing. He brushed his best—and only—suit of rusty black. Then he checked himself in the broken mirror that hung in the school.

Ichabod wanted to make his appearance before his lady like a true knight. So he borrowed a horse from the farmer he was staying with. This man was a cranky old Dutchman named Hans Van Ripper.

---

[12]The Roman god Mercury is a messenger. He wears a winged cap to speed him on his way.

[13]Here and in a later passage, Irving crudely stereotypes blacks.

Riding in this gallant style, Ichabod set out like a knight in quest of adventure. But in the true spirit of romantic stories, I should give some account of how my hero and his horse looked.

The animal Ichabod rode was a broken-down plow horse. This horse had outlived almost everything but meanness. He was thin and shaggy. He had a short neck and a head like a hammer. His rusty mane and tail were tangled and knotted with burrs.

One eye did not have a pupil. It was glaring and spectral. The other had the gleam of a real devil in it.

Still, the horse must have had fire and spirit in his day. That is if you can judge from his name, Gunpowder. In fact, he had been a favorite horse of his master's, the cranky Van Ripper.

Van Ripper was a furious rider. He had probably filled the animal with some of his own spirit. As old and broken-down as the horse looked, he had more of the devil in him than any young horse around.

Ichabod was a suitable rider for such a horse. He rode with short stirrups. This brought his knees nearly up to the top of the saddle. His sharp elbows stuck out like a grasshopper's. He carried his whip straight up like a staff. As his horse jogged on, his arms flapped like a pair of wings.

A small wool hat rested on the top of his nose. At least I suppose you could call his scanty forehead that. The bottom of his black coat fluttered out almost to the horse's tail.

That was how Ichabod and his horse looked as they shambled out Hans Van Ripper's gate. Altogether, it was such a sight as you will seldom see in broad daylight.

It was, as I have said, a fine fall day. The sky was clear and calm. Nature wore that rich, golden uniform which we associate with abundance. The forests had put on their sober brown and yellow. Some tender trees had been nipped by the frosts. They had turned brilliant dyes of orange, purple, and scarlet.

Streaming files of wild ducks began to appear high in the air. The squirrel could be heard in the beech and hickory trees. The sad whistle of the quail came from the nearby fields at times.

The small birds were eating their farewell feasts. They fluttered, chirped, and frolicked from bush to bush and tree to tree. Their number and variety made them playful.

There was the robin, with its loud, angry notes. Young sportsmen love hunting the honest robin.

There were also the twittering blackbirds flying in dark clouds. The golden-winged woodpecker with his red crest, black throat, and splendid feathers was there, too.

The cedar bird flew past as well. Ichabod could see its red-tipped wings, yellow-tipped tail, and little cap of feathers.

And the blue jay, that noisy fellow—Ichabod saw him. He was in his bright light-blue coat and white underclothes. He screamed, chattered, nodded, bobbed, and bowed. He was pretending to be on good terms with every singer in the woods.

Ichabod jogged slowly on his way. As usual, his eye was open to every sign of abundant food. So he surveyed the treasures of jolly fall with delight as he rode.

On all sides he saw huge supplies of apples. Some were hanging in heavy richness on the trees. Some were gathered into baskets and barrels for the market. Others were heaped up in big piles for the cider machine.

Farther on he saw great fields of Indian corn. The golden ears peeped from their leafy hiding places. They held out the promise of cakes and hasty-pudding.

Yellow pumpkins lay beneath the corn. Their pale, round bellies were turned to the sun. They gave **ample** signs of making delicious pies.

Soon Ichabod passed the good-smelling buckwheat fields.

He breathed in the odor of the beehives. As he gazed at them, he imagined dainty flapjacks. He pictured them well buttered and topped with honey or molasses by Katrina's delicate little hand.

Thus Ichabod rode on, feeding his mind with sweet thoughts and "sugared hopes." He journeyed along the sides of hills. Here you could see some of the prettiest views of the mighty Hudson.

The sun gradually wheeled its broad disk down into the west. The wide Tappan Zee lay mostly motionless and glassy. Sometimes a gentle wave stirred or lengthened the blue shadow of a distant mountain.

A few yellow clouds floated in the sky. There was not even a breath of air to move them.

The horizon was a fine golden tint. It changed gradually to a pure apple green and then to a deep blue. A slanting ray lingered on the wooded cliffs that hung over the river. This ray made the dark gray and purple of the rocky slopes look even deeper.

A ship was lingering in the distance, slowly moving with the tide. Her sail hung uselessly against the mast. The reflection of the sky gleamed in the still water. It seemed the vessel hung in the air.

Toward evening Ichabod arrived at the castle of Mr. Van Tassel. He found it crowded with the pride and flower of the adjacent countryside. He saw the old farmers—a lean, leather-faced race. They wore homemade coats and pants. On their feet were blue stockings and huge shoes with magnificent pewter buckles.

The brisk, wrinkled little wives of the farmers were there, too. They wore caps, long-waisted short gowns, and homemade petticoats. Scissors and pincushions dangled from ribbons as decorations. Bright pockets hung on the outside of their gowns.

The blooming girls were almost as old-fashioned as their

mothers. The only signs of newer city styles were a straw hat, a fine ribbon, or a white frock here and there.

The sons were in short, square-tailed coats with rows of huge brass buttons. Their hair was generally fixed in a pigtail, as was the fashion. They especially did this if they could get an eel skin to tie back their hair. It was esteemed everywhere for strengthening hair.

However, Brom Bones was the hero of the scene. He had come to the gathering on his favorite horse, Daredevil. Like Brom, this creature was full of spirit and mischief. No one but Brom himself could manage Daredevil.

In fact, Brom was noted for preferring vicious animals. He liked ones who pulled all kinds of tricks and constantly risked the neck of the rider. Brom thought an obedient, well-broken horse was unworthy of a lad with spirit.

I would love to pause and dwell upon the charms that met my hero's gaze as he entered Van Tassel's parlor. I do not mean the flock of blooming girls in their ample display of red and white.

No, I mean the plentiful charms of a genuine Dutch tea table in fall. There were such heaped-up platters of cakes of various and almost endless kinds! Only the experienced Dutch housewives knew them all.

There was the sturdy doughnut, the tenderer oly koek pastry, and the crisp and crumbling cruller. There were sweet cakes and short cakes, ginger cakes and honey cakes. In fact, the whole family of cakes was on the table.

Then there were apple pies, peach pies, and pumpkin pies. Slices of ham and smoked beef filled several plates. And there were delicious dishes of plums, peaches, pears, and quinces. Not to mention the broiled fish and roasted chickens, along with bowls of milk and cream.

Everything was mixed together in a helter-skelter way, pretty much as I have said. In the middle sat the motherly teapot. It was sending up its clouds of steam.

Heaven help me! I need breath and time to discuss this feast as it deserves. But I am too eager to get on with my story. Fortunately, Ichabod Crane was not in so great a hurry as this storyteller. He did ample justice to every dainty on the table.

Ichabod was a kind and thankful creature. His heart swelled the more his skin was filled with good food. His spirit rose with eating as some men's do with drink.

He could not help, too, rolling his eyes around him as he ate. He chuckled at the possibility that he might one day be lord of this scene. What incredible wealth and splendor!

Ichabod thought then how soon he'd turn his back on the old schoolhouse. He'd snap his fingers at Hans Van Ripper and all the other cheap farmers who housed him. Just let a wandering teacher try to call him friend. Ichabod would kick him out the door!

Old Baltus Van Tassel moved about among his guests. His face was filled with contentment and good humor. It looked as round and jolly as the harvest moon.

Baltus' greetings were brief but friendly. He would shake a hand, slap someone on the shoulder, or laugh loudly. And he would always press his guests to "dig in and help themselves."

Now the sound of music from the hall summoned people to the dance. The musician was an old gray-haired Negro. He had been wandering orchestra of the neighborhood for more than half a century.

The man's instrument was as old and battered as he was. Most of the time he scraped on two or three strings. With every move of the bow, he moved his head. He would bow almost to the ground and stamp his foot to signal when a fresh couple should join in.

Ichabod was as proud of his dancing as of his singing. Not one of his limbs or nerves was idle. His loosely built frame in full motion, clattering about the room, was quite a sight. You would have thought Saint Vitus, that blessed saint of the dance, was before you.[14]

Ichabod was admired by all the Negroes. A group of all ages and sizes from the neighborhood had gathered. They stood forming a pyramid of black faces at every door and window. They gazed at the scene, wide-eyed with delight.

How could this beater of lads be anything but lively and joyous? His lady love was his dance partner. And she was smiling kindly in reply to all his amorous glances.

Meanwhile, Brom Bones sat brooding by himself in a corner. He was overcome with love and jealousy.

When the dance was at an end, Ichabod was attracted to a group of wise folk. Along with Van Tassel, they sat smoking at one end of the porch. They were gossiping about old times and drawing out long stories of the war.

At the time of the story, the valley was one of those lucky places filled with tales and great men. The British and American line had run near the valley during the revolutionary war.

Therefore, the area had been the scene of raids. People seeking safety, cowboys,[15] and all kinds of chivalrous people had filled the area.

Just enough time had passed for each storyteller to dress up his tale with a little fiction. And, with the blurring of memory, they could turn themselves into the heroes of every event.

There was the story of Doffue Martling, a large blue-bearded Dutchman. He had attacked a British ship with a small old cannon. He might have captured the ship if the cannon had not burst at the sixth shot.

And there was an old gentleman who shall remain

---

[14]People prayed to this Christian saint to cure diseases that caused twitching and jerking.
[15]Cowboys were Americans on the British side who secretly fought near New York City during the Revolution.

nameless. He is too rich a fellow to be mentioned lightly. He said that he was at the battle of White Plains.[16]

As an excellent master of defense, he had blocked a musket ball with a sword. He felt it whiz round the blade and bounce off the handle. To prove it, he was always ready to show the sword with its bent handle.

There were several more who had been equally great in battle. Each one seemed convinced that he played a large part in bringing the war to a happy end.

But all these stories were nothing compared to the tales of ghosts that followed. The neighborhood is rich in such legendary treasures. Local tales and superstitions last longest in these old, sheltered retreats. But they are trampled underfoot by moving crowds in most of our country places.

Besides, ghosts do not have much of a chance in most villages. They scarcely have time to finish their first nap and turn in their graves before their live friends have moved away.

Therefore, when the ghosts get up, they have no friends to call on. This may explain why we so seldom hear of ghosts except in our oldest Dutch towns.

But the real reason why there were so many supernatural stories was that Sleepy Hollow was in the vicinity. There was a germ in the very air that blew from the haunted region. It infected all the land with an atmosphere of dreams and fancies.

Several of the Sleepy Hollow people were present at Van Tassel's. As usual, they were serving up their wild and amazing legends. Many **dismal** tales were told about funeral mourners. They also told of cries and wails heard and seen near a huge tree close by. This was the tree where the unfortunate Major Andre[17] was seized.

---

[16]White Plains was the site of a Revolutionary battle near New York City.
[17]Major John Andre (1751-80) served in the British army during the American Revolution. He was caught scheming with the American traitor, Benedict Arnold. Andre was put on trial and hanged.

Some mention was also made of the woman in white. She haunted the dark valley at Raven Rock. She was often heard to shriek on winter nights before a storm. She had died there in the snow.

But most of the stories were about the favorite specter of Sleepy Hollow—the headless horseman. He had been heard several times lately, patroling the country. It was said that he tied his horse every night among the graves in the churchyard.

The out-of-the-way location of this church had always made it a favorite place for troubled spirits. It stands on a little hill, surrounded by locust trees and tall elms.

From among those trees, its whitewashed walls shine out modestly. They look like symbols of Christian purity beaming through the quiet shadows.

A gentle slope runs down from the church to a silver sheet of water. This lake is bordered by tall trees. Between their branches, you can catch peeps of the blue hills of the Hudson.

In that grassy churchyard, the sunbeams sleep quietly. You would think the dead would rest in peace there.

On one side of the church stretches a wide woody valley. Along that valley runs a large brook among rocks and fallen tree trunks.

Over a deep black part of the stream not far from the church, a wooden bridge once stood. The road that led to it and the bridge itself were thickly shaded by trees. Even in the daytime, these trees cast a gloom. But at night, they caused the path to be fearfully dark.

This was one of the favorite places of the headless horseman. In fact, it was the place where he was most often met.

A tale was told about old Brouwer. He was a great unbeliever when it came to ghosts.

Brouwer met the horseman returning from his trip into

Sleepy Hollow. The horseman made Brouwer get on the horse behind him. Then they galloped over bush and ferns, over hill and swamp, until they reached the bridge.

There the horseman suddenly turned into a skeleton. He threw old Brouwer into the brook. Then he sprang over the treetops with a clap of thunder.

This story was immediately matched by an amazing adventure Brom Bones had. Brom joked that the galloping Hessian was an out-and-out cheater.

Brom swore that one night on his way from the village of Sing Sing, this midnight trooper had overtaken him. Brom had offered to race with the horseman for a bowl of punch.

He would have won the bet, too. Daredevil was beating the goblin horse soundly. But just as they came to the church bridge, the Hessian fled. He vanished in a flash of fire.

These tales were told in the drowsy, low tone with which men talk in the dark. The faces of the listeners were dark. Only now and then were they lit up by a stray gleam from a pipe.

The stories sank deep into Ichabod's mind. He repaid them in kind with many **extracts** from his beloved author, Cotton Mather. And he added accounts of marvelous events that had taken place in Connecticut. He told, too, of things he had seen on his nightly walks about Sleepy Hollow.

The party now gradually broke up. The old farmers gathered their families into their wagons. They were heard for some time rattling along the roads and over the hills.

Some of the girls rode double behind their favorite young men. Their lighthearted laughter and the clatter of hoofs mingled. The echo of this sound traveled along the silent woods. The sound grew fainter and fainter until it died away.

Finally the scene which had been so noisy and frolicking was all silent and deserted.

Ichabod only lingered behind to have a heart-to-heart talk with Katrina. Such was the custom of country lovers. He was fully convinced that he was now on the road to success.

What passed during their meeting, I will not pretend to say. In fact, I do not know. But I fear that something must have gone wrong. Ichabod came out after a rather short time with quite a sad and downfallen look.

Oh, these women! These women! Could that girl have been playing any of her flirty tricks? Did she only pretend to encourage the poor teacher in order to win his rival?

Heaven only knows—I do not! I will only say that Ichabod crept out like one who has been stealing hens rather than a lovely lady's heart.

He did not look to the right or left at the rich countryside over which he had so often gloated. Instead, he went straight to the stable. With several hearty slaps and kicks, he rudely woke up his horse. Old Gunpowder had been sound asleep. He had been dreaming of mountains of corn and oats and whole valleys of grass and clover.

It was exactly the witching hour when Ichabod set out. Heavyhearted and downfallen, he made his way home. He rode over those same hills above Tarrytown which he had traveled so cheerily that afternoon. The hour was as dismal as he was.

Far below him, the Tappan Zee spread its dark waters. The tall mast of an anchored ship could be seen here and there.

In the dead hush of midnight, Ichabod could even hear a watchdog barking on the other shore. But the sound was vague and faint. It only showed him how distant was this faithful friend of man.

Now and then the crowing of a rooster would sound, too. But it came from far, far off on some farm among the hills. It was like a dreaming sound in his ear.

There were no signs of life near Icahbod. But occasionally he heard the sad chirp of a cricket. Sometimes it was the deep twang of a bullfrog from a nearby marsh. The frog's croak sounded like it had just turned suddenly in its bed.

All the stories of ghosts and goblins that Ichabod had heard earlier now came rushing into his mind. The night grew darker and darker. The stars seemed to sink deeper in the sky. Blowing clouds occasionally hid them from his sight.

Ichabod had never felt so lonely and dismal. Moreover, he was nearing the very spot where many of the ghost stories had taken place.

In the center of the road stood a huge tulip tree. It towered like a giant above all other trees nearby. Indeed, the tree formed a kind of landmark.

The limbs of the tree were knotted, weird-looking, and large enough to form the trunks of ordinary trees. These branches twisted down almost to the earth before rising again into the air.

The huge tree was connected to the tragic story of the unfortunate Andre. He had been taken prisoner close by. Everyone knew the tree by the name of Major Andre's tree.

The common people regarded the tree with both respect and superstition. This was partly out of sympathy for the unlucky man it was associated with. But it was also partly from the strange sights and sad moaning reported near the tree.

As Ichabod approached this fearful tree, he began to whistle. He thought his whistle was answered. But it was just a blast sweeping through the dry branches.

As Ichabod came nearer, he thought he saw something white hanging in the tree. He paused and ceased whistling. But on looking closer, he saw that it was a white spot where the tree had been scarred by lightning.

Suddenly he heard a groan. His teeth chattered and his knees knocked against the saddle. But it was just the rubbing of one huge branch against the other as they swayed in the breeze.

Ichabod passed the tree safely. But new dangers lay before him.

About two hundred yards from the tree, a small brook crossed the road. It ran into a marshy and thickly wooded valley called Wiley's swamp. A few rough logs, laid side by side, served as a bridge over this stream.

To pass this bridge was the hardest test. It was at this same spot that the unfortunate Andre had been captured. The farmers had hidden to ambush him under the cover of those chestnuts and vines.

Ever since then, this has been considered a haunted stream. The schoolboy who has to pass it alone after dark is filled with fear.

As Ichabod approached the stream, his heart began to thump. However, he summoned up all his courage. Then he gave his horse about ten kicks in the ribs and tried to dash briskly across the bridge.

But the stubborn old animal did not go forward. Instead, it made a **lateral** move and ran smack into the fence.

Ichabod's fears increased with the delay. He jerked the reins and kicked hard with his other foot.

It was all in vain. His horse started, it is true. But it only plunged to the opposite side of the road into some bushes.

The schoolmaster now used both the whip and his heels on Gunpowder's skinny ribs. The horse did dash forward, snuffling and snorting. But he stopped just by the bridge so suddenly that he nearly threw off his rider.

Just then, Ichabod caught the sound of a splashing, tramping noise by the bridge. He saw something in the dark shadow by the brook. It was huge, misshapen, black, and towering.

This shape did not stir. It just seemed cloaked in the gloom like some gigantic monster ready to spring.

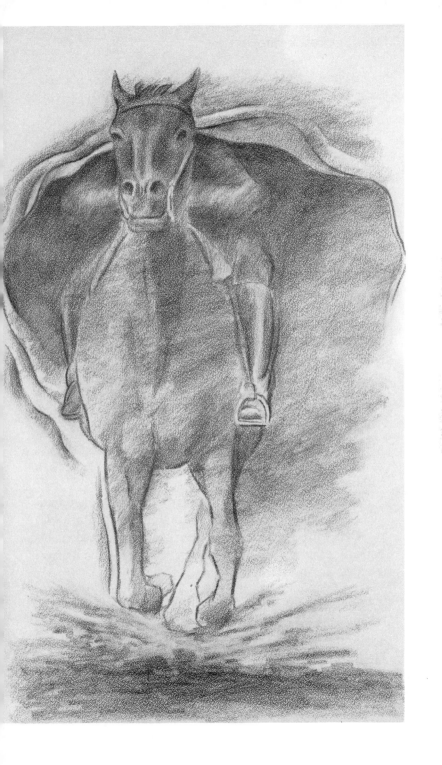

The hair of the frightened teacher rose up on his head with terror. What was to be done? It was too late to turn and flee.

Besides, what chance was there of escaping a ghost or goblin, if it was that? They could ride upon the wings of the wind.

Therefore, Ichabod summoned up a show of courage. With a stammer he demanded, "Who are you?"

He received no reply.

He repeated his demand in a voice that shook even more. Still there was no answer.

Once more Ichabod beat the sides of the unmovable Gunpowder. Shutting his eyes, he began singing a hymn with great feeling.

Just then the alarming, shadowy object moved. With a scramble and a bound, it now stood in the middle of the road.

Though the night was dark and dismal, the form of the stranger could now be seen better. He appeared to be a giant horseman mounted on a powerful black horse.

He did not try to attack or greet Ichabod. Instead he jogged along on one side of the road next to Gunpowder's blind side. The old horse had now gotten over its fright and stubbornness.

Ichabod did not like the company of this strange midnight companion. He recalled Brom Bones' adventure with the Galloping Hessian. So he quickened the speed of his horse, hoping to leave the horseman behind. But the stranger speeded up to match Ichabod.

Then Ichabod slowed his horse down to a walk. He hoped to lag behind. But the other did the same thing.

Ichabod's heart began to sink. He tried to sing his hymn again. But his dry tongue stuck to the roof of his mouth. He could not utter a stanza.

There was something in the moody silence of this determined companion that was mysterious and ghastly. Ichabod soon saw the reason for this. When Ichabod's fellow traveler rode to the top of a hill, he could be seen against the sky.

Ichabod saw that the horseman was a giant in height and wrapped in a cloak. But he was horror-struck to see that the horseman was headless!

Ichabod's horror grew when he observed that the horseman carried his head before him on the saddle!

Ichabod's terror became desperation. He rained a shower of kicks and blows upon Gunpowder. He hoped by a sudden movement to give his companion the slip.

But the specter started out in full stride with Ichabod. Away then they dashed through thick and thin. Stones flews and sparks flashed at every leap.

Ichabod's flimsy clothes fluttered in the air. He stretched his long, skinny body over his horse's head in his eagerness to flee.

They now reached the road which turns off to Sleepy Hollow. But Gunpowder seemed possessed by a demon. He did not continue on. No, he made an opposite turn and plunged headlong downhill to the left.

This road leads through a sandy valley. It is shaded by trees for about a quarter of a mile where it crosses the famous goblin bridge. Just beyond rises the green hill where the church stands.

As yet, Gunpowder's panic had given his unskillful rider an edge in the chase. But just as Ichabod got halfway through the valley, his saddle straps gave way. He could feel the saddle slipping from under him.

Ichabod seized the front of the saddle and tried to hold it firm. But it was in vain. He just had time to save himself by grabbing old Gunpowder round the neck when the saddle fell to earth. Ichabod heard it trampled underfoot by the headless horseman.

For a moment, the terrors of Hans Van Ripper's anger passed across his mind. It was Van Ripper's best saddle.

But this was no time for petty fears. The goblin was hard on his heels.

And unskillful rider that he was, Ichabod was having great trouble staying on the horse. Sometimes he slipped to one side, sometimes to the other. Sometimes he jolted on the horse's backbone so hard that he feared he would be split in two.

Ichabod saw an opening in the trees. He began hoping that the church bridge was nearby. The wavering reflection of a silver star in the brook told him that he was not mistaken. He saw the church walls dimly glaring upon the trees.

Ichabod recalled the place where Brom Bones' ghostly companion had disappeared. "If I but reach that bridge, I am safe," thought Ichabod.

Just then he heard the black horse panting and breathing close behind him. He even imagined that he felt its hot breath.

With another sharp kick in the ribs, Gunpowder sprang upon the bridge. He thundered over the echoing planks. Then he reached the opposite side.

Now Ichabod cast a look behind. He wanted to see if the horseman would vanish in a flash of fire and brimstone, as usual.

Just then he saw the goblin rise up in his stirrups. He was in the very act of hurling his head at Ichabod!

Ichabod tried to dodge the horrible missile. But he was too late. It hit his head with a tremendous crash.

Ichabod tumbled headfirst into the dust. Gunpowder, the black horse, and the goblin rider passed by like a whirlwind.

The next morning the old horse was found without his saddle and with the bridle at his feet. He was calmly eating the grass at his master's gate.

Ichabod did not appear at breakfast. Dinner came, but no Ichabod. The boys gathered at the school and strolled idly by the brook. But no schoolmaster.

Hans Van Ripper began to feel some uneasiness about the fate of poor Ichabod and his saddle. An investigation was set in motion.

After a **diligent** search, they came upon his traces. On the road leading to the church was found the saddle trampled in the dirt. Tracks of horses' hoofs deeply dented the road. They seemed to have been going at a furious speed. These tracks were traced to the bridge.

Beyond that, near where the water ran deep and black, was found unlucky Ichabod's hat. Close beside it was a shattered pumpkin.

The brook was searched. But the body of the schoolmaster was not discovered.

Hans Van Ripper was left to take care of Ichabod's belongings. He examined the bundle which contained all of Ichabod's worldly goods. They consisted of two shirts and a half, two scarfs, a pair or two of stockings, an old pair of knickers, a rusty razor, a dog-eared book of hymns, and a broken pitchpipe.

As to the books and furniture of the school, they belonged to the community. Ichabod's only property was Cotton Mather's *History of Witchcraft, a New England Almanac*.

There was also Ichabod's book of dreams and fortunetelling. In that one was a sheet of paper with many scribbles and blots. Ichabod had tried several times in vain to write a poem in honor of Katrina.

The magic books and poetic scrawl were immediately burned by Hans Van Ripper. From that time on, he determined he would never send his children to school again. He said that he never knew any good to come out of this reading and writing.

The schoolmaster had received his quarterly pay just a

day or two earlier. But whatever money he still had he must have been carrying with him when he disappeared.

The mysterious event caused much discussion at the church on the following Sunday. Knots of gazers and gossips collected in the churchyard. They stood at the bridge, at the spot where the hat and pumpkin had been found.

The stories of Brouwer, Bones, and a whole flock of others were recalled. They had diligently considered them all and compared them to the present case. Then they shook their heads. They came to the conclusion that Ichabod had been carried off by the Galloping Hessian.

As Ichabod was a bachelor and in nobody's debt, nobody worried about him any more. The school was moved to a different place in the Hollow. Another teacher ruled in his place.

It is true that an old farmer who told me this ghostly tale said he heard that Ichabod Crane was still alive. The farmer had been down to New York on a visit several years later. He brought back the following news of Ichabod.

It seemed Ichabod left partly through fear of the goblin and Hans Van Ripper. He also left because he was shamed at having been suddenly dismissed by Katrina.

Ichabod had supposedly moved to a distant part of the country. There he taught and studied law at the same time.

He eventually became a lawyer. Then he turned politician, ran for office, and wrote for the newspaper. Finally he was made a judge in small claims court.

Shortly after his rival disappeared, Brom Bones led the blooming Katrina in triumph to the altar. He looked very knowing whenever the story of Ichabod was told. And he always burst into hearty laughter at the mention of the pumpkin. This led some to suspect that he knew more about the matter than he chose to tell.

However, the old country wives are the best judge of these matters. They maintain to this day that Ichabod was carried off by supernatural means. It is a favorite story often told about the neighborhood round the winter evening fire.

The bridge became more than ever an object of superstitious fear. That may be the reason why the road was changed recently. Now it approaches the church by the border of the millpond.

The empty school soon fell into decay. It was reported to be haunted by the ghost of the unfortunate teacher.

The plowboy, lingering on a still summer evening, has often fancied he heard Ichabod's voice at a distance. He seemed to be chanting a sad hymn in the quiet loneliness of Sleepy Hollow.

"The Legend of Sleepy Hollow" was first published in 1820.

INSIGHTS INTO
WASHINGTON IRVING

(1783-1859)

In 1809, strange ads appeared in the newspapers. The first ad noted that an odd man named Diedrich Knickerbocker had vanished.

The next ad noted that Knickerbocker's landlord had found a book by his renter. The landlord said he would publish the book to make up for rent money still owed him.

Soon after, *Knickerbocker's History of New York* was published. This comic book of history was a wonderful success.

The real author of the book and the ads? Washington Irving.

Diedrich Knickerbocker was just one of Irving's faces. He wrote under a number of names to capture a style or make a joke. Jonathan Oldstyle, William Wizard, Anthony Evergreen, and Geoffrey Crayon were some of his pen names.

For a long time, Irving did not settle down in earnest to any career. He passed the bar. But he was never an energetic lawyer.

Then Irving tried to help save part of the family business in England. After three draining years, the firm went bankrupt.

The bankruptcy was a secret blessing. Lack of money and hatred for business led Irving to devote himself to writing. His only gift to business was a phrase he coined: "the almighty dollar."

Irving's work helped shape the modern short story. Plus, he did what no American before him had done. He earned the respect of European critics.

Thackeray, a famous British novelist, was one who praised Irving. He called Irving "the first Ambassador from the New World of Letters . . . to the Old."

In the late 1830s, Irving bought an old Dutch farmhouse. In a way, living at Sunnyside was a return home for Irving. The house had been owned by relatives of some real Van Tassels. And it was located in the very region where "Sleepy Hollow" had been set.

Other works by Irving:

"Adventure of the German Student," short story
"Rip Van Winkle," short story
"The Spectre Bridegroom," short story